Searching for Rachel

A novel by

Richard Standring

Richard Standring

Also by Richard Standring

HUSTLE (1989)
  Electronic Media Network, Inc.

DANGEROUS DANCING (2000)
  Xlibris Corp.

DANGEROUS RELATIONSHIPS (2001)
  Infinity Publishing

DANGEROUS ENCOUNTERS (2003)
  Infinity Publishing

SOMEWHERE ALONG THE WAY (2004)
(*a collection of short stories, poems & essays*)
  Instant Publishing

VANISHED (2004)
(*a short story appearing in the anthology,*
Stories of the Unexpected*)
  Publish America

Richard Standring

Copyright © 2007 Richard Standring
(Mystery, Detective, Fiction)

ISBN: 978-1-60458-105-8

This is a work of fiction. None of the names of people mentioned are real. Any resemblance is accidental and only the places actually exist. To help readers, who want to refer back to a given named character, I've included an *Index of Characters* at the end of this novel.

The author wishes to thank Sharon Templeton and Marcia E. Brine for their help, encouragement and proofreading the manuscript for errors. I take full credit for any mistakes that remain. If, as you read this story, you should discover a typographical error, just smile and read on, as I often do when reading other authors' work.

Special thanks to all my past reading fans for their suggestions and encouragement. I truly appreciate your continued support.

Richard Standring

Chapter 1

Nick Alexander was on his way to Center Hill Lake, to look around, maybe find a nice piece of property for sale at a price he could afford. With any luck, perhaps he'd even find something with a lake view, or better yet, with a lake access. Every time he visited middle Tennessee, he planned on spending a day to explore the lake area, and for once, he had the time to spare.

He was thinking about a model log home he'd visited a month ago, and how he might modify the floor plan, when he heard a siren and looked into his rearview mirror. Flashing lights were behind him so he pulled over, still unaware that the police car was actually following him.

"License and registration please," the deputy said, standing beside the open driver's window. "And take the license out of the wallet," he added.

"Sure, but may I ask why I've been pulled over?" Nick asked.

"Guess you didn't see the sign back there. Speed limit is fifty-five."

"And how fast did you have me clocked?"

"Got you at fifty-nine point six. It's easy to pick up speed on this downhill section."

"You stopped me for going fifty-nine in a fifty-five zone? Must be a slow day." Nick was having trouble keeping his temper from showing. He flashed his private investigator badge as he handed over his license. Then he reached across the seat to open the glove box, for the registration.

"Open that slowly, son. No fast movements, understand?"

Nick decided it was his Michigan license plate. Anyone local wouldn't have been stopped for going downhill at 59 miles per hours on a bright sunny afternoon, with no traffic to speak of. It was a four-lane highway leading down to a bridge that crossed over the lake and continued on into Smithville. It still annoyed him when men younger than he was, called him "son". Even though he knew it was just a southern expression.

"I know the drill. I've done it many times when I was still in uniform."

"Uh huh, but you ain't a police officer any more are you? And you sure as heck aren't in Michigan, unless yer lost."

Nick didn't see any point in giving out additional details, or arguing. He just waited while the deputy returned to his patrol car. Nick tapped a silent cadence with his fingers on the steering wheel while he waited, trying to regain some composure. He should have known better than to be so preoccupied that he hadn't monitored his speed. Never the less, this was ridiculous. He wondered what the fine would amount to.

"Okay Mister Alexander. You'll need to sign this ticket stating that you'll appear in court on the twenty-third of this month. Or you can pay the fine before then at the court house. Fine's forty-five dollars by the way."

Searching for Rachel

Nick signed the ticket, kept his copy and noted the deputy's name, Randy Cooper. He heard the deputy say, "Y'all have a nice day now, hear?"

Well it was a nice day, until now. He wasn't going to let the incident mar his mission. It never occurred to Nick that he might meet the deputy again, as well as the sheriff, later that day, under different circumstances.

While Nick was exploring secondary roads around Center Hill Lake, Sheriff Bobby Joe Hanks was busy reviewing an old missing person's report:

Rachel Greene *was missing for forty-eight hours before a missing persons report was filed with the DeKalb County Sheriff's Department.* This wasn't just some teen-ager who decided to run off to be with undesirable friends for some weekend fun. This was a married woman; a mother and the daughter of rich parents, who also lived in Smithville, Tennessee. *She was reported missing by her parents, Ezra and Maureen Rueben, not by her husband, Barry.* The sheriff was re-reading his notes, reviewing all the details for what could easily be the two hundredth time. *Rachel's parents became concerned when they hadn't heard from their daughter by Sunday evening. This was most unusual, because they spoke at least once or twice every day, according to the mother. And, they were watching their only grandchild, Jonathan, while Rachel and Barry spent the weekend on the family's houseboat on Center Hill Lake.* The lake being just north, and east, of Smithville put it in the sheriff's jurisdiction, keeping his office busy during the summer.

Sheriff Bobby Joe Hanks had all these facts in his computer, plus some personal observations. It bothered him that Barry didn't appear overly concerned about

Rachel's disappearance, and he'd made a note to himself about that. It was another of many sore points with Rachel's parents. *Barry told his in-laws, "they'd had an argument" and, that Rachel left Sunday afternoon saying, "She needed some time alone".* This was Barry's justification for not having notified the police of her disappearance. *Given time to cool off, he felt certain she'd return.* During one of many interviews, the sheriff noted that *it annoyed Barry that his in-laws were so quick to involve the police. Barry indicated they were always a bit too judgmental when he was involved.* According to Barry, he'd tried numerous times to come to grips with their attitude toward him and finally concluded it was a losing situation. Despite the fact that Barry was Jewish, he still wasn't part of the family. The sheriff thought the Jews always favored their own. It didn't help that Barry worked for Ezra and was under the man's constant scrutiny. The sheriff tried to keep an open mind about Barry, however, he felt Ezra had every right to be concerned about his daughter's disappearance. At one point, Barry was his prime suspect.

Sometimes the sheriff wished his office wasn't on the town square and therefore just a short block away from Ezra's Smithville real estate branch office. Being that close, meant Sheriff Bobby Joe had the distinct pleasure of having Ezra breathing down his neck more frequently than he liked. It still bugged him when Ezra took it upon himself to hold a press conference, without ever consulting him. The man's impatience could wear you out, he thought to himself.

Sheriff's Deputy Randy Cooper's report established that Rachel Greene was last seen leaving the Hurricane Marina on Sunday afternoon in her red Mercedes convertible. The top was down. Odell Hickey, a dock attendant at the marina, stated he saw her depart the houseboat and drive away, leaving her husband stranded at the marina. Apparently there was an argument. The attendant did not know what the argument was about. This information was also in the sheriff's computer. Rachel no doubt had her father's temper.

Rachel Greene had red hair, making it easy for Odell to identify her. *Allegedly, Barry Greene remained on the houseboat Sunday evening, and left on Monday morning, after calling an associate at work to pick him up. He was seen leaving the marina on Monday morning. Nobody could vouch for his remaining on the houseboat Sunday evening.* If you weren't driving, it was a very long walk to almost anywhere since the marina was somewhat isolated. It was a sure bet Barry wouldn't call his in-laws for a lift home.

Rachel Greene's Mercedes convertible was later discovered in long-term parking at Nashville International Airport, with the top up. The sheriff estimated that it was about a forty-five minute drive to the airport, provided traffic was light. She'd no doubt drive west partway on Interstate 40 and get off at the airport exit. *Checking on departure flights, police learned that a Rachel Greene purchased a one-way ticket to New Orleans, using her Visa card that same Sunday.* That was a real puzzler. The sheriff wondered once again, why she hadn't purchased a round-trip ticket? A one-way ticket suggested she wasn't planning to return anytime soon. Sheriff Bobby Joe, and his department, were secretly relieved that Rachel Greene's whereabouts had shifted out of their jurisdiction to New Orleans. It meant fewer visits, and phone inquiries, from Ezra. Despite the time lapse, he still showed up periodically.

The New Orleans trip also removed Barry as a suspect. It still annoyed the sheriff that the man didn't display more concern, regardless of his relationship with his in-laws.

The sheriff could recall times when he didn't get overly enthused, when he learned that his mother-in-law was coming for a visit. Staying more than a day was too long. His wife always waited until the very last minute to tell him she was coming. Then she'd add, "Don't you remember, I mentioned this to you last week." He knew he wasn't that forgetful, particularly when it involved her visits.

Scrolling down the computer screen, the sheriff re-read a notation, that *earlier that Sunday afternoon, in late July, Rachel apparently bought six gallons of gas at a local fuel stop on Highway 70 just outside Smithville, on her way to the airport. They knew that because the fuel slip, stamped with the time and date, was found on the floor of her car.* Now wasn't that a convenient piece of evidence. Had it not been for the marina attendant's statement, the sheriff would still be looking at Barry as a suspect. He could have planted that receipt. It was a mystery that continued to bother the sheriff. Enough so that at least once a week he'd review all the notes in the computer, looking for something he might have missed. He felt certain she wasn't kidnapped, since a ransom never materialized.

The search for Rachel Greene had shifted to New Orleans, where she apparently vanished. *No hotel or motel registrations were found under Rachel Greene's name. No one matching her description had registered at any of the better accommodations. And, no other charges were made using her Visa card. She just disappeared, without leaving a trace.*

The sheriff knew New Orleans could be a dangerous place for an attractive woman, traveling alone. Crime statistics listed New Orleans high on the chart for violent crimes. It had gotten even worse recently. The charm and mystique were still there, along with a growing number of homeless people. He'd heard the shelters were full and overflowing.

Searching for Rachel

For the New Orleans police, the sheriff knew that Rachel would be just another of hundreds of currently missing women. As a normal routine, he knew they checked all the hospitals and the morgue, in case of an accident. A bulletin was posted with a recent photo that would eventually find its way to all the post office lobbies. Rachel Greene would be yet another face among hundreds, if not thousands missing. An overburdened police force wasn't capable of conducting an intense search. Their search routine was restricted to just the basic procedures.

The sheriff knew, just like the New Orleans Police Department knew, some of the missing became homeless street people who didn't want to be found. Mostly these were druggies. They joined the growing nameless masses in New Orleans, a magnet for the lost and those who wanted to hide. It had always been that way.

The tedious task of posting the information was about all anyone could expect from the police, considering the overwhelming number of new bulletins coming in every day. The sheriff knew The Big Easy was known for having a unique slow pace. Most things got done eventually, and in their own time. Faster, is a request one makes to a taxi driver, not to public servants. Sheriff Bobby Joe felt fortunate that he'd been able to get as much information as he had from the New Orleans police. They'd actually been very cooperative, surprising him.

If Rachel Greene didn't want to be found, she picked one of the better places to disappear, he thought. Why she'd left was the real question.

The sheriff remembered one interview when *Barry said that Rachel called him at home on Tuesday evening, around 7:00, saying that she was staying in New Orleans for a few days and asked him to tell her parents, and to ask them to keep their son for a few additional days. A check of phone records confirmed that a collect phone call from*

Richard Standring

New Orleans to the Greene's Smithville home did occur on Tuesday evening at 7:13. Once again, this seemed to be just a little too convenient. Why wouldn't she have called her mother instead? Was this whole thing a big insurance scam? He'd checked and learned there were large amounts of insurance on all three: Barry, Jonathan and Rachel. Ezra hadn't mentioned the amount.

Rachel's call was traced to a pay phone at the bus station in downtown New Orleans. None of the ticket people at the bus station recalled selling a ticket to anyone fitting Rachel's description, according to the report the New Orleans police sent the sheriff. This was actually more police attention than most missing person cases received. *No attempt was made to question any of the waiting taxi drivers.*

That was six months ago, and Rachel Greene hadn't been seen, or heard from, since.

The sheriff was well aware that Rachel's parents were convinced that their son-in-law knew more about her disappearance than he had so far revealed. *They suspected he was involved and speculated that he had perhaps killed her and hidden her body somewhere. Yet no evidence of foul play was found to confirm that suspicion.* Therefore, the sheriff didn't have sufficient reason to hold Barry as a primary suspect. However, the sheriff continued to keep him listed as a person of interest.

Sheriff Bobby Joe didn't have a lot of experience with cases like this one. He was a small-town sheriff used to dealing with small-town problems. He still relied heavily on his gut instincts. He knew bad, when he smelled it. And Barry Greene had a peculiar foul odor about him.

Knowing that Ezra Rueben would most likely stop by the sheriff's office around lunchtime, at least once a week, was cause enough to be out of the office, just before the lunch hour began. Usually Ezra stopped by on a Friday, making the man somewhat predictable. Sheriff Bobby Joe sympathized with the man's situation, but without something new to report, there just wasn't anything to talk about. And he disliked being reminded that Ezra had donated a substantial amount of money to his re-election fund.

Mentioning it once would have been enough.

Chapter 2

Ezra Rueben's background was well documented. Most people were aware of the man's success. He'd built a real estate empire in Nashville and surrounding communities, including Smithville. He owned several shopping malls and had nine real estate offices, one of which his son-in-law, Barry managed in Smithville, on the square, not more than 150 yards from the sheriff's office. If the sheriff had played a fair game of golf, he could have easily hit it easily using a 5-iron. He sometimes lamented the close proximity.

The sheriff suspected the Smithville office wasn't the most productive in the group because it was obviously the smallest of the nine. It was the office where Barry worked, and it was close to where Barry and Rachel lived. For that matter, it was also close to where Ezra and Maureen lived. Both lived only five miles away, to the east of town and overlooking the southern portion of the lake.
Consequently, Ezra frequently showed up at the Smithville office on Friday afternoons, on his way home from Nashville.

Everyone knew that Ezra was a shrewd businessman, respected for his early vision, turning nearby farms into high-priced gated communities around Nashville for the country music giants.

Searching for Rachel

Rachel was his only child and the sheriff could recall Ezra admitting to spoiling her and his only grandson, Jonathan. He also openly admitted that he never truly approved of Barry. *When Ezra learned that Barry and Rachel were seriously considering getting married, he had hired a private investigator to check out Barry's background.* This didn't surprise the sheriff. He knew Ezra was naturally suspicious and highly protective of his family, his reputation and his wealth. *Ezra was convinced that Barry pursued his daughter, knowing that she was an only child from a wealthy family. Ezra openly admitted that he considered Barry to be a cunning gigolo with an appetite for money and a secure future.* That's the picture Ezra painted of his son-in-law. Was it an attempt to sway the sheriff's opinion? Probably. Being a good Southern Baptist, Sheriff Bobby Joe was careful not to express his opinions about Ezra's religious background. A quick sideways glance at one of his deputies was sufficient to keep casual remarks and slurs in check. Jews were definitely a minority in this part of the state. If Ezra wanted to attend services he'd have to drive to Nashville. Most folks in Smithville were either Baptist, Church of Christ, or Sunday golfers and fishermen.

The wedding between Rachel and Barry happened seven years ago.

Now, after six months, without any word, or evidence of where Rachel might be, Ezra used his influence to rekindle media coverage of her disappearance. *A $100,000 reward was offered for information leading to her discovery.* Had he been asked, the sheriff would have advised against offering such a large sum. All it did was prompt a lot of crazies to call his office and waste his time. Ezra also insisted the sheriff conduct another extensive search of the grounds surrounding Rachel's and Barry's home. The sheriff felt it was a waste of time and man power, but complied in the interest of being cooperative, particularly since the case had gained some national media attention. That's what money, serious money, could do for you, he thought. He hated to admit that money could manipulate, and even ruin, people. Ezra was certainly trying to ruin Barry in an act of revenge.

The property they searched overlooked Center Hill Lake from a high vantage point, making a search of the area difficult as well as time-consuming. Parts were heavily wooded. *Neither the house, nor the surrounding area outside provided any clues as to what may have happened.* This didn't come as any surprise to the sheriff.

Several days were spent digging, prodding and searching the surrounding wooded areas, all to no avail. The deputies, as well as some local volunteers, knew the effort was just an exercise, to indulge a prosperous citizen who supported the sheriff's re-election campaign. It was agreed among the deputies involved that since Rachel Greene flew to New Orleans, on a one-way ticket, there was no need to be searching the nearby woods around the lake. The search needed to focus in and around New Orleans. The sheriff suspected that as a result, the search effort became rather haphazard just to indulge Ezra's wishes. Anyone who knew Center Hill Lake knew that a comprehensive search was nearly impossible with over 400 miles of shoreline involved.

It was annoying to watch Ezra appearing on Nashville television offering a reward and, during the interview with a local television reporter, hinting that Barry was somehow involved. Nothing was mentioned of Ezra's and Maureen's attempt to get custody of their only grandson. The sheriff suspected it was a separate issue being pursued quietly. He'd heard a few rumors. Those who knew Ezra also knew the man always seemed to have a hidden agenda. Sheriff Bobby Joe's re-election hinged on Ezra's support, so he had to keep his annoyance hidden, even in his computer notes.

The sheriff kept his opinion of Ezra to himself. Yet it was difficult to keep from rolling his eyes whenever one of the deputies would announce that Ezra was on the phone. He knew that Ezra was a self-made millionaire. Just how much he was worth was anyone's guess. The sheriff also knew Ezra was highly opinionated, domineering, impatient and demanding. He was suspicious of everyone outside his immediate family. His grandson was the primary focus of the man's devotion. The sheriff had heard a rumor that money had been put into long-term bank CDs to pay for the boy's future college education soon after the boy was born. No doubt Ezra probably changed his will to include his grandson in the family fortune. Would Barry ever know about that, he wondered.

The problem the sheriff had with Barry was primarily a matter of motive. Just suppose Barry and Rachel were having problems. Why would Barry be stupid enough to want Rachel dead? It just didn't make any sense. The smarter thing to do would be to file for divorce, and let the old man buy him off, if money was Barry's main objective. Murder, if it really was a homicide, was never a good solution to any problem, not that he'd investigated that many murders. Those he had, all involved robbery or drugs. So everything was pure speculation and everyone seemed to have an opinion, but no proof.

In DeKalb County, farmers didn't murder their wives. They just wore them out instead, he mused. Sheriff Bobby Joe and his wife, Eunice were about to celebrate forty years of marriage and there had been some rough periods, when he used to drink. Sure, they'd argued, but he'd never laid an angry hand on her. Harsh words were different, they could be taken back, and he'd done his share of apologizing. So the fact that Barry and Rachel had been arguing, and that she'd left without him, didn't by itself constitute much to worry about, at first. It was her long absence, without any contact with her family, that bothered him. It suggested that she was dead. It was a gut feeling. *Jonathan would no doubt go to Vanderbilt University in Nashville, where Ezra and Rachel also attended college. Barry wouldn't have a vote in that decision, which was probably already made. Jonathan's educational destiny was already pre-determined. So Barry didn't have to worry about that future expense. Perhaps Barry felt resentful of being kept out of the decision loop. Not having a vote might cause some resentment.* The sheriff ruminated over all these various bits and pieces of information he'd gleaned since Rachel's disappearance.

Then something totally unexpected happened....

A stranger walked into the sheriff's office, presented his business card and announced he was working for Ezra Rueben. The card indicated his name was Nick Alexander, Private Investigator with a Michigan address.

"So what brings a big-city investigator to our parts, Mr. Alexander," the sheriff said, turning from the computer.

"My girlfriend lives in Cookeville, and I've been coming down here for the past four years. In fact, I worked a case in Cookeville a few years back."

"And how is it you happen to know Ezra Rueben?"

"Well, it's really strange how all this just suddenly happened." Nick went on to relate how he'd been driving around Center Hill Lake checking out land for sale. For the past year, he'd been considering a permanent move to Tennessee. And since he liked to fish, the lake area looked inviting. He'd heard about the famous Bass tournaments. When he stopped by the local real estate office, he met Ezra, who just happened to be there, since it was Friday,

Searching for Rachel

and Ezra just happened to see Nick's business card, because he was nosey. That in turn led to Ezra asking Nick if he'd had any experience with missing persons. Nick explained he had a lot of experience, having been a homicide detective with the Saint Clair Shores Police Department, before retiring to start his own business. That business was doing background checks on key employees who worked for companies that had government contracts, or the company was concerned about industrial spying. It was a departure from Nick's previous police activity. He missed some of the previous excitement, but not the danger it posed.

The sheriff sat back and took full measure of the man standing before him. He thought he looked a lot like the actor, Richard Geer. Same full head of graying hair, with an intense look, even when he smiled. The man appeared to be about six feet tall, give or take, and trim. The sheriff estimated he was in his late fifties. Rather than grill him about his credentials, he'd wait and check him out later, and get a full report.

"And just what is it we can do for you, Mr. Alexander?"

"Please, call me Nick. And, I've always found it easier to talk sitting down, if that's all right with you, sheriff." Nick didn't want to remain standing, looking down at the sheriff. It wasn't good body language.

"Sorry, I should have told you to rest your bones sooner. I'm just curious how you managed to suddenly show up here on my doorstep." Obviously Ezra sent him over. "I'm a bit surprised he didn't call me first, to tell me you were coming," he added.

"That's because I just left him at the office, and since you're so close, I decided to walk over and introduce myself. Sometime when it's convenient, I'd like to review your case reports on Rachel's disappearance." Nick was trying to be as friendly as possible, knowing the sheriff didn't have to cooperate. Ezra had assured him the sheriff would, so there was an element of leverage, but he hoped it wouldn't be necessary.

"I'm not all that sure it will do you much good. Rachel disappeared in New Orleans. That's probably where you should be looking, not here."

"You may be right, but I'd still like to get a complete over view of all the events leading up to her disappearance. Once I have it all sorted out, I'll no doubt make a trip down to New Orleans."

Deputy Randy Cooper had been standing in the doorway, listening. He'd been busy filing reports and didn't notice the man when entered earlier to see the sheriff.

"Hey Coop why don't you come on in. This here's Deputy Cooper. He's the one who has been my right arm in the investigation here." The sheriff didn't bother to add that Randy was also his nephew, and in time would be the next sheriff when Bobby Joe retired. "Say hello to Nick Alexander from Michigan. I reckon St. Clair Shores is somewhere around Detroit." Nick wasn't sure if that was a question, or a statement.

Nick turned around and nodded. "I believe we've already met earlier." Without his hat, the deputy looked to be in his early thirties and prematurely balding. He was showing a little bulge around his waist. Nick wondered if that was the beginning of a beer gut. "Deputy Cooper was working the speed trap north of town and clocked me going fifty-nine on the downhill grade, just before the bridge."

"That so? He give you a warning, or a ticket?"

"I was expecting a warning, but I guess you folks need the money."

"Not that bad, we don't. Coop, kill the ticket for God's sake." He turned back to Nick, "Since you've just been hired by Ezra, I take it you don't know much about him. Be prepared to give him detailed reports of all your activity, every day. Don't leave anything out, either."

"It's not the way I usually work. I gather from your comments that he'll be a little difficult."

"Oh yeah, you'll earn your money."

Money hadn't been Nick's primary motive for accepting the assignment. He had a barter arrangement in mind, but that didn't have to be anything he had to discuss with the sheriff.

In the interest of keeping Ezra off his back, the sheriff decided to print out the official reports he had in the computer, leaving out his personal notes. He gave Nick a copy and wished him good luck.

"I expect you to keep me posted on your progress," the sheriff added as Nick left.

"Hey sheriff, what's that slicker going to find that we don't already know?" Deputy Cooper asked. He'd remained standing.

"You just never know what he might turn up. If it keeps Ezra from calling me all the time, I'm good with it. Here's his card, run a check on him. I'd like to know a bit more about this Nick Alexander. He told me he's staying in Cookeville with his girl friend. Her address and phone number are written on the back of the card." It was the sheriff's opinion that it never hurt to have a lot of background information on people involved in an ongoing investigation. And, you could never be too careful when strangers, particularly Yankee strangers, showed up. It seemed they brought along their own brand of trouble.

Chapter 3

Carol Mayberry was delighted when Nick told her that he would be sticking around a while longer. He had only planned to remain in Cookeville another day, before heading down to Atlanta, where he had a waiting assignment. Now, his plans were changed. Even though he lived just outside Detroit, and she lived in Cookeville, they saw one another as often as possible, and talked just about every day on the phone. It was coming up on ten years since Nick had been divorced. He and Carol had been an item for the last four years, though it seemed longer than that. He couldn't imagine what life would be like without her. She had the ability to make his sour moods vanish. Perhaps it was her exceptional cooking ability. Whatever it was, he would never get enough. Some of that good cooking translated into added calories,
 forcing him to activate his old routine of running five miles every morning.

"So what's this Ezra Rueben like?" Carol asked. "I've seen his name in the newspaper."

"He's sort of flinty. Reminds me a little of what Abraham Lincoln must have looked like, without a beard. He's about my height, but leaner. Looks like an undertaker in that black suit he was wearing. He said that he and

Searching for Rachel

Rachel played tennis at least twice a week. And, I gather from the sheriff, he's on the demanding side. I'll need to explain a few things to him tomorrow, after I've talked with a few people and looked around."

"His daughter's disappearance has been in the news a lot. Nick, do you really think you can be of some help?" Carol was happy that Nick would be staying longer. "After all, it's been a few months since she disappeared."

Carol and Nick had a special relationship and a deep love for one another. As a widow, Carol never thought she'd ever fall in love again. She never even thought about it, until she met Nick. At the time, she'd was executive secretary to the president of a local furniture manufacturing company. When her boss died, he left Carol some stock in the company. Later, she was promoted to general manager because of her extensive knowledge and persuasive manner. Nick had been hired by the company to do background checks on key employees. It was a requirement, because the company had a big government contract, making furniture for embassy offices. Since then, she and Nick had been seeing one another as much as possible, even taking vacations together. Carol felt that the time would come when Nick would ask her the big question, and when he did, she had her answer ready. Meanwhile, every day, and night, they spent together was a bonus, in her opinion.

"It's too early to answer that. After I've read everything in the sheriff's report, I'll have a better picture of what I'm dealing with." He was coming into a cold case. The woman had been missing for seven months. He doubted that she'd still be alive. Regardless, her parents had a right to know what had happened and possibly why. It wasn't going to be easy.

Nick spent the rest of the evening reading and re-reading all the reports making notes. He made a list of the people he wanted to interview, starting with the marina attendant, Odell Hickey. That's where the mysterious disappearance began.

Ezra had given Nick a set of keys to the houseboat along with a card, and his cell phone number. It had all happened so fast that Nick hadn't even bothered to mention his fee. Based on what he knew so far, it wasn't going to be a problem... unless Nick couldn't produce some results. Something in the back of his head told him that this assignment was going to be a difficult challenge. Here he was, a Yankee in red neck territory, trying to get answers to a mystery that was already a cold case.

What he had in mind, was a little bartering for a piece of land. Ezra knew the area better than anyone, and the man owned a lot of property. Maybe some sort of trade-off could be worked out. That was Nick's primary reason for taking the assignment. Perhaps someday, he'd build a nice, modern-style log house near the lake where he and Carol could spend the rest of their days together.

That was a dream he had yet to discuss with Carol. Naturally he'd consult with her before he had anything built. He'd made enough mistakes in his first marriage and he didn't plan to make those same mistakes again. Lust and sex had been his primary motives for getting married then. Now it was friendship, and sex was still important, but not in the same way. Add mutual understanding and respect. All those things added up to an ideal arrangement. Nick knew he was lucky to have found a woman like Carol; a woman with good morals, a strong character and a great sense of humor. She rarely disagreed with Nick, and he couldn't remember when they'd had an argument, if ever. The looming question was, would getting married again change their relationship? He hoped it wouldn't. It was the primary reason he'd held off asking. He didn't want anything to change. If she wanted, Carol could keep her

Searching for Rachel

last name rather than to change it to Alexander. It would be her choice.

Nick called his client in Atlanta and explained that he would be delayed for an unspecified period. In his absence, he'd called a friend, who helped on larger projects, to fill in. Keeping all his clients happy was essential when you were in a competitive line of work. Just about all of Nick's assignments came to him in the form of recommendations from other clients. It was something he was particularly proud of.

Chapter 4

Odell Hickey was fueling a boat when Nick arrived at the marina. He waited until the man was finished before attempting to talk with him. Nick used the extra time to observe the man. He was wearing faded jeans and a worn plaid shirt with long sleeves that covered his arms. He appeared to be in his late fifties, but Nick knew that determining someone's age could be a problem in this area, where people were sun-baked, prematurely wrinkled and victims to smoking and chewing tobacco. A forty-year old could look sixty. In parts of West Virginia and Kentucky it was equally difficult. Miners and their wives lived hard lives and it showed.

Nick introduced himself and presented his business card. When they shook hands, Nick could feel the man's calloused hands. In preparation for today's visit, Nick also wore jeans and an open sports shirt plus a tan and orange Tennessee Vols ball cap Carol had given to him to wear when he played golf. He hoped it would help shed the Yankee image and make Odell feel a bit more comfortable.

"I already told that deputy, Randy something what happened. I was here working when their houseboat came back that Sunday afternoon. That houseboat's a big sumbitch and not easy to dock, either. I gave 'em a hand with the ropes and helped guide it in. Next thing you know, she's yelling something and jumps to the dock and heads for that fancy car of hers, and drives off, stirrin' up a lot of dust. That's about it. I reckon she was pissed about somethin'. I hear redheads are like that."

"And nobody else was around that time of day?" Nick asked.

"Oh I suppose so, but nobody close by."

"Any idea what they were arguing about?"

"Nope. I heard her shout somethin' like, 'I don't care what you do'."

"Uh huh, and you knew this was Mrs. Greene because ...." Nick waited.

"Well for one thing, I've seen her here before with her daddy and the kid. She's a good lookin' red head. Kinda hard to miss."

"She didn't say anything to you on the way to her car?"

"Nope. Marched right by, got in and put the top down and drove off."

"Do you recall what she was wearing that day?"

"Mister, I'm tellin' you she was a looker. Had on them big sunglasses, looked like a movie star. I didn't notice much else. No sir." He'd also noticed her beautiful breasts bouncing up and down, but didn't feel the need to mention it.

"So you didn't notice any bruises, or anything like that?"

"Like I just said, I saw what little there was of her face, and what I saw sure looked pretty. You ask me, that husband of hers has got it made, marrying into a rich family, gettin' full use of the old man's houseboat anytime he wants, and havin' a sexy little wife like that. Lots of people would sure be willin' to trade places." Suddenly an empty cola can materialized and Nick watched the man spit into the can. "I'll tell you what, I may be old, but I know pretty when I see it."

Nick noticed that Odell had a missing tooth when he smiled. The rest were badly stained.

"Did you happen to see them arrive together?"

"Yep. I helped him untie the houseboat, unplug the electric and asked him if there was anything else he needed. He tipped me five bucks. I remember that."

"Do you recall what she was wearing the day they arrived?"

"Can't say as I do. She sort of disappeared into the houseboat as soon as they arrived. Didn't help with the lines."

"Did anyone else arrive, or go with them?"

"Nope. Just the two of them, alone. Someone came and got him the next morning. I think it was someone from his office, a younger guy in a Jeep."

"So Mr. Greene spent Sunday night alone on the houseboat in the slip?"

"As far as I know. I saw the lights on. Didn't see him go anywhere. Of course he could have taken a walk and I wouldn't have noticed. I'm not here all the time, just seems like it."

"So, which one of these big houseboats belongs to Ezra Rueben?" Nick had keys. It turned out to be one of the largest in the marina. It looked like a floating palace. Nick wondered how one person could maneuver such a large craft without a crew. He would be happy to stay aboard and remain at the marina, not going anywhere.

He was familiar with houseboats because he'd had a similar case four years ago, involving another woman's disappearance. For a brief moment, Nick flashed back to that event. It was a different marina, but still on Center Hill Lake, where the woman had been abducted. Eventually, they found her body buried in a shallow grave, covered

Searching for Rachel

with bricks and an old tarp, on her ex-husband's farm in Jackson County. The jealous ex-husband had stalked and later abducted her. Nick hoped this wouldn't be a similar type incident. In that case, the missing woman had worked for Carol's company, and Carol knew her, making it all the more gruesome.

This houseboat was about the same size as the one the furniture company used to own. They'd used it for entertaining clients. Later, when Carol became the interim general manager, she sold it and put the money into some needed new equipment in the plant, which was a very smart move. Every time Nick thought about Carol, he was amazed at the woman's insight and capacity for logic. None of the share-holders ever had to worry about how the company was being managed with Carol at the helm. Her honesty and capability were well-known by those who knew her. The caring side was a slightly different Carol, and equally appreciated by Nick.

He was her number one fan, and she was his. They had the ideal relationship and it worried Nick that it might change, if they ever got married. It wasn't something that either of them discussed. They sort of talked around the subject, neither of them wanting to disturb the harmony they currently shared.

As Nick worked his way through the vessel, he couldn't find any evidence of a struggle, nothing was broken or out of place. No signs of blood anywhere. Nick wondered if anyone had even bothered to check out the houseboat. At best, it would have been routine procedure, since it was the point of departure in the case. Nick didn't see any evidence of fingerprint powder. When he was still a homicide detective, it would have been an early request as a matter of standard investigative procedure.

For just a moment, Nick was back on the force hearing someone ask him, why was that necessary? Why?

Because it always helped to know who had been there. By checking every little detail, even when it didn't seem relevant, helped him solve some past difficult cases. It was those little, easily over-looked items that eventually led him to the truth. He was always reminding the other officers that for any homicide to be successfully prosecuted, there had to be a well-defined, easily understood motive. Jurors didn't respond well to speculation and suggested scenarios. Opportunity was another item that needed to be well-established. And, of course there had to be a corpse, with the cause of death also well-established by a professional medical examiner. Without these three essentials, police didn't have a case worth presenting to a jury.

None of those elements were present here. It looked like the houseboat could be eliminated as a crime scene. No doubt the sheriff had made the same conclusion. He had to be careful not to be critical of how the sheriff handled things.

This case was still at the puzzle stage. Six months ago, Nick would have been able to get more accurate recall of events leading up to the day Rachel disappeared. The basic techniques still applied, however. You went back to the starting point and worked your way through the sequence of events, never assuming too much. Always listening for what people *weren't* telling you, and watching their body language for lies and evasiveness. It was another reason Nick disliked telephone interviews. The eyes could tell a lot.

He had to be careful not to be too influenced by what Ezra thought. Keeping an open mind around that man would be difficult. He had a way of forcing his opinions on you with great intensity. Trying to say no, in a real estate negotiation, would be next to impossible, Nick thought. Perhaps it was an asset to the man. Certainly it was part of his demeanor. The man had armor plate for skin. For a moment, Nick could almost feel a modicum of pity for the son-in-law who had to put up with him on an ongoing basis.

Nick did a second walk through. He had a feeling he was overlooking something. In one of the guest staterooms he opened a closet door and noticed four folded blankets neatly stacked, sitting on the floor. Why not in a cabinet drawer, or shelf, he wondered?

Looking in the far corner of the closet, he spotted what appeared to be a large tray with a divider of some sort standing on end. It reminded him of the inserts he'd seen in old steamer trunks. Yes, that's what it was. Turning around, Nick inspected the floor carefully. He saw a slight indentation in the carpet where a piece of furniture was placed at one time. It was easy to overlook, if you didn't know what you were looking for. The carpeting on the houseboat wasn't as plush as some homes. It wasn't a deep impression, like from a heavy piece of furniture. It could have been a trunk. The size was right.

Nick took a picture of the stacked blankets in the closet, a picture of the tray and another of the indentations, and then placed the tray over the area. The geometry of the indentation matched the tray. Nick estimated the dimensions to be approximately 24" by 48". If it wasn't a trunk, it had to be a dresser, but a dresser would leave just marks where the four supporting feet were. This was a continuous depression. If someone removed the trunk, why didn't they also remove the insert? Perhaps it was an oversight, just the kind of mistake a person makes when they are rushed and not thinking clearly. Nick was fairly certain he'd discovered an important clue; one everyone else had missed... if they even bothered to look.

He guessed the blankets were stored inside the missing trunk. It would be the perfect place to keep them. Perhaps it was now at the house. Nick made a mental note to look for it there. Ezra might not know about something like a missing trunk in a guest stateroom, but Mrs. Rueben would surely know, if she spent any time on the houseboat. Ezra indicated that he rarely used the houseboat, so he might not remember certain items missing, particularly from rooms he wouldn't normally occupy or visit.

So far, Odell's comments tracked with the police report.

Nick took digital pictures of the houseboat inside and out. Next on his list was the house Barry and Rachel lived in. Mrs. Rueben might have a set of keys. And it would give him a good excuse to interview her, about her daughter, and get a list of Rachel's friends. She'd no doubt be a better source than Ezra, he thought.

Chapter 5

Maureen Rueben already knew that Ezra had hired yet another private investigator. This wasn't the first, and she doubted it would be the last. She wasn't surprised when she saw Nick park in the drive. Earlier, over breakfast, Ezra had hinted that someone named Nick Alexander might call, or stop by.

Nick took his time getting out and walking to the front door. He was admiring the big house with stone accents, numerous roof angles, and massive picture windows that afforded an exceptional view of the lake below. There was a circular drive as well as another drive beside the house, leading back to a four-car garage and swimming pool beyond. The house was displayed in the middle of manicured landscaping. It was difficult for Nick to determine the lot size, since the lawn was surrounded by tall pines. Neighboring houses couldn't be seen. It was totally private and quiet, except for an occasional bird call. Carol had mentioned that he might see some eagles in the area.

Nick was surprised when Mrs. Rueben answered the door. A wire hair terrier was beside her, wagging its tail. He was half-expecting a maid.

Maureen Rueben was dressed casual. She wore a flower patterned top, that went below her waist, partially covering the top of her white slacks. *Probably designed to disguise a heavy waistline*, he thought. Her deeply-tanned feet were bare inside expensive leather sandals. At one time, this was a very attractive woman, Nick decided. Still could be, if she lost about 40 pounds. Obviously she wasn't into exercising like Ezra or Rachel. Nick doubted that she played tennis. Looking out the French doors in the back of the house he noticed a fenced-in tennis court behind the huge in-ground swimming pool.

Nick perceived a loneliness in the woman, much like people who are mourning a loved one who recently passed away. And perhaps that was the case, he thought. She had a pleasant, but distant smile. She didn't maintain any eye contact. Instead, she'd look off toward the lake and talked in a different direction, as if talking to herself while petting the dog.

"Tell me about Rachel," Nick thought a soft beginning was the best way to handle this woman. Maureen sat on a leather sofa opposite Nick in a matching sofa. She'd placed glasses of iced tea and cookies on a tray sitting on a coffee table between them. It served as a subtle buffer zone. The dog's name was Jake and he sat obediently beside Maureen while eyeing the coffee table.

"She was the love of our life and the center of our attention from the very beginning, when she was born. We spoiled her, just as we're now spoiling our grandson. That is, whenever we get the opportunity. He's living with his father in Ocala right now."

"I see." Nick didn't want to ask too many questions. He just wanted her to ramble in whatever fashion suited her. He'd learn a lot more that way.

"I'm not sure how much my husband has told you, or how much you already know, but Barry has been a big disappointment in all this mess. Ezra is sure he knows a lot more than he's revealed so far. Getting anything out of him has been like pulling teeth. When he and Rachel got married, he was the sweetest man. Ezra had his doubts from the very beginning, but I didn't. Rachel loved him and he was good to her. He was ambitious and I thought Ezra would admire that quality. The fact that Barry was ten years older than Rachel didn't bother me, but I think it, how can I say this... it kept him from being closer with some of Rachel's friends whose husbands are younger. I don't think Barry had much in common with them."

"Could you provide me with a list of her friends?"

"Of course. Oh my, where was I? Lately I'm having trouble remembering things and I don't sleep as well as I used to."

"That's understandable. Is Ezra having similar experiences?"

"If he is, he's doing a good job of keeping it to himself. Ezra rarely exhibits any emotion, even when he's angry, you'd never know it."

"Well, he's certainly a successful businessman from what I've heard."

"Oh yes, he's always been that way." Maureen went on to tell Nick about their early days together, when they'd gotten married just after college. Her parents were the ones with all the money. She said Ezra was enamored with her family's social position. She said her father owned a recording company in Nashville and had helped many famous musical artists get started. When he died, his estate went to Maureen. Like Rachel, she was an only child. Her inheritance was enough to help launch Ezra's first shopping mall venture. Now, she enjoyed all the benefits of her husband's success and eventual wealth. She had hoped something similar might happen with Barry and Rachel.

"How did Barry and Rachel meet?"

"You probably won't believe this. As a graduation present, Ezra wanted to get Rachel something special, something she always wanted. That something was a new sports car. She saw one in a dealer show room that she really liked. It was a BMW. Barry worked at that dealership and was the salesman who sold the car. Shortly after that, he started calling Rachel asking how the car was, and if she wanted to go out with him."

"So he was a car salesman. How did he get into real estate?"

"That was my idea, after they became engaged. I suggested that it might be nice if Ezra could find a place for him in one of the offices, maybe in Nashville, since he lived there. Barry took real estate courses and worked for another real estate broker for a little while to get his license. I think that impressed Ezra and he hired him." Ezra probably wanted to keep an eye on him, Nick thought.

"Was he any good at selling real estate?"

"I think he was. Ezra isn't the kind of person who passes out much praise, but he did admit that Barry was doing better than expected. After he and Rachel got married, Ezra made him the manager of the Smithville office so he'd be closer to home. We gave them that land as a wedding present and helped with the down payment on the house. Rachel designed it just the way she wanted it. She has a good eye for things like that. She's a talented artist, too, in case Ezra didn't mention it." She pointed to several paintings on the walls.

"It's convenient they were living so close to you."

"Oh yes, that was part of the plan. Ezra and Rachel could play tennis out back, whenever it was cool. She and Jake jogged around this area every morning. And we could practically walk over to their house to see the baby." Nick couldn't picture Maureen walking that far.

"It sounds like the ideal set up. What happened to change things?"

"I truly believe that part of the problem was our fault, but Ezra will never admit that. We were always very close as a family. Rachel would come over, or call at least once and sometimes twice a day. We'd talk about a lot of things."

"Did she ever mention having problems with Barry?"

"She told me that Barry was becoming annoyed that we saw so much of each other. He didn't like it that we were spoiling Jonathan. He said we were interjecting ourselves into their life too much and smothering them."

For a moment, she thought back to the time she and Ezra had bought Jake for Jonathan. Nobody had mentioned it to Barry beforehand. When they showed up with the dog, Jonathan was so pleased, but not Barry. He'd been kept out of the decision, only Rachel knew about it.

"Do you think that was the source of their last argument?"

"I believe so, yes. Of course it could have been anything. Barry was beginning to irritate Ezra at work. I don't know if Ezra was deliberately pushing him too hard, or if it was something else. Ezra is used to having things go his way. Some of Barry's suggestions didn't sit too well with him."

"I guess that's the price one pays for working in the family business. If Barry was unhappy, why didn't he just leave and find another position with another company?"

Nick was making mental notes, not writing anything down. He'd learned years ago, that people talked more freely when it wasn't a formal interview with notes being taken, or a recording.

"That's a very good question. Perhaps it's because he was making good money working for Ezra and couldn't match it elsewhere. I don't know. I do know that Ezra pushed a little too hard when he went on television and practically accused Barry of having something to do with Rachel's disappearance. It forced Barry to leave. And of course he took Jonathan with him. It broke my heart to see my darling grandson leave here. I don't think Ezra completely anticipated that. And, as you can see, they didn't take Jake with them. He's Jonathan's dog. We bought Jake for Jonathan for his fourth birthday. Jake misses Jonathan almost as much as we do. Poor thing is always looking out the window, waiting for Jonathan. And he misses the walking. Rachel liked to walk. She'd take Jake with her when she went."

"I'm not trying to be judgmental Mrs. Rueben, but I can see where anyone in Barry's position would feel awkward remaining in Ezra's employment, after being accused like that. He probably thought he had no choice, he had to get away from the constant scrutiny." Nick hadn't planned to mention what Barry might have been thinking. And, having not met the man, he should wait a while longer before making those judgments.

"I suppose you're right. At any rate, we've lost Rachel and now we've just about lost Jonathan. If only we knew where Rachel was, and if she was still alive. Ezra believes she's dead. I haven't given up hope. It upsets me that she hasn't tried to reach me somehow."

Nick had to agree. If the mother and daughter were that close, why wouldn't she tell her mother she was leaving and give her the where and why? A mother wouldn't just leave her son like that, either.

"That painting was one of her more recent pieces." Maureen pointed to the wall beside the fireplace. "Ezra has another in his Nashville office. She's very talented don't you think?"

"I agree." Nick got up to examine the painting up close.

"Is it possible that Barry pursued your daughter because she was rich and married her for the money he hoped would follow?"

"I've thought about that. I honestly think Barry loved Rachel. He'd do the cutest things, when they were dating. He'd come to the house to pick her up, and later, I'd discover a box of my favorite Godiva chocolates hidden somewhere, where I'd eventually find them. Barry knew that was one of my weaknesses."

"So he buttered you up."

"Well, isn't that what good sales people do when they want to make a big sale, or a good impression?"

And it worked, Nick said to himself, just nodding in agreement. Eventually he'd get around to meeting Barry and making some determinations on his own.

"Is the house currently vacant?" Nick wanted to go through the place and spend some time there alone.

"Yes, it's just the way Barry left it. Rachel's Mercedes is parked in the garage. The battery is probably dead by now. The electricity is on because of the alarm system and because we want the furnace to keep working on cold days. We have a maintenance company take care of the lawn. We won't sell the house until we know for sure that Rachel isn't coming back."

"What about mortgage payments. Is Barry making those?"

"Heavens no! Before he left, we paid off the mortgage. We could have done that sooner, but Ezra.... Well never mind about that." She didn't finish and Nick suspected that she didn't want to say anything that would put Ezra in a bad light, like trying to control and manipulate a situation.

"When was the last time you were on the houseboat?" Nick asked.

"Let me see, it's been a while. Certainly not since Rachel left us."

"I noticed a tray, like a trunk insert, in one of the closets and there was a stack of folded blankets on the floor. I was wondering if they might have been stored in a trunk of some sort. Do you recall anything like that?"

"Hmm, no I don't. Oh yes, I bought an old trunk two and a half years ago for Jonathan's play room, so he could keep his toys in it. I seem to remember Rachel taking it to the houseboat to store blankets. Isn't it there now?"

"Perhaps it's back at the house, but I didn't see it anywhere on the houseboat."

Maureen gave Nick the list of friends he asked for, along with two recent photos. One photo was of Rachel. The other was a family picture of Barry, Jonathan and Rachel. Both were in color. Nick had to admit, it was an attractive family. She gave him the keys to the house, along with the code for the alarm system.

"I hope you won't mind if I should need to call you. I'm sure there will be questions I haven't thought to ask."

"You can call here any time. And I'm sure you'll be in touch with Ezra on a regular basis. I'll tell him you were here today."

Maureen watched the private investigator leave and wondered if he might actually discover something useful; something the others had overlooked. He'd asked about the trunk. Nobody else had mentioned it. Perhaps Barry took it with him when he left. She picked up her glass of ice tea and walked out to the patio, with Jake, who was getting excited at the prospect of going outside, where he could run around the yard.

The private investigator's visit caused her to reflect on some of her earlier discussions with Rachel about Barry. There was a time when Maureen found herself being just a

Searching for Rachel

bit jealous of their romantic relationship. The only passion Ezra ever exhibited was toward making more money. He was never charming in the way Barry was. Making love was a rare and brief moment. She often wondered if Ezra thought of it more as a duty than a lustful urge. Having separate bedrooms didn't help, although she had to admit she never heard Ezra snoring, and he didn't hear her crying. He never knew how lonely she'd become now that Rachel was gone.

Everyone envied her because she had everything anyone could possibly want: They had a part-time cook and housekeeper so Maureen never had to step foot into the kitchen, except to get something from the refrigerator. A landscape service took care of everything outside. Sometimes out of boredom she'd do a load of wash, but she never had to iron anything. Some days she felt like a queen locked away in a distant castle. Reading, particularly gothic romance novels, had become her escape from reality.

Ezra rarely entertained, and when he did, it was always at the country club, never at the house. Maureen would agree to show up, but didn't have much interest in joining business discussions. She left that up to Ezra, knowing they were more than financially secure, regardless of market conditions. She disliked most of the gushy people who pretended to be friends. Ezra was good at indulging the phonies, because he used them when it suited him. He explained that it was all part of doing business and she was glad to be removed from it. Coming from a wealthy family, perhaps she'd always been a bit removed, or was it sheltered? She decided it was all about money, power and greed. She was happy to be removed from all of it. She refused to be part of the superficial society scene. They no doubt consider me a snob, she thought. And I guess I just don't care what they think, she mused.

Whatever Ezra lacked in affection, he more than made up for it with security and she accepted that as her fate. Divorce wasn't, and never would be, a consideration. So why then had Rachel seen fit to just walk away from everyone? Was her life really that bad? Maureen had tried to understand what her daughter might have experienced that she'd never mentioned. Maureen couldn't think what it could possibly be. It wasn't as if she'd refused to discuss certain things with Rachel. Sometimes she felt foolish talking to Jake about all her frustrations.

Rachel and Barry's house was larger than Nick expected it to be, but not nearly as large as the one he'd just left. The drive sloped down from the street so that the garage was under the house and the basement had a walk out to a large patio that overlooked a dense crop of trees and the lake beyond. The main floor had a huge deck that extended over part of the patio below. Nick spent a half hour walking around the house and yard outside. The lot looked to be at least two acres, with the nearest neighbor 200 yards away. Barry and Rachel could have a good shouting match and no one would hear a thing. For that matter, someone could arrive or leave un-noticed, unless they just happened to be walking by. Nick doubted the neighbors would have seen much.

There was evidence that police had been there digging in various areas in the back yard beyond the patio. The lake could be seen between stands of pines and it was possible to walk down to the water if you were careful. It was a steep slope 50 feet beyond the patio with a stand of pine trees partially blocking the view.

Nick considered what he'd do if he owned this place, he'd have a small pier down there with a small run-about, ready to go whenever he wanted to fish, or just feel the breeze on a hot afternoon. He knew that pontoon boats

Searching for Rachel

were a popular choice of water craft for family fun on inland lakes like this. However, they were not good if you were in a hurry to get someplace. It was Nick's secret wish to one day own a classic, old open cockpit Chris Craft or Garwood. He'd seen a few and often wondered what it would be like to skip across a glassy lake in one, creating a wide wake as he swung around in a wide circle. He knew something like that was beyond his means, but it was still a nice dream. *Had Barry played his cards right, he might have had one.*

If Ezra had been his father-in-law, and his wife had disappeared, Nick doubted that he'd leave as Barry had done. Leaving wasn't the answer to the problem, unless Barry was just using that to punish Ezra, knowing how much they'd miss Jonathan. And, he hadn't taken the boy's dog along. Maybe he'd left it as a daily reminder of the consequences.

Nick spent two hours examining the interior of the house and taking more pictures. It was a four-bedroom home with a studio and skylight for Rachel's painting. Several of her pieces hung on walls in the hallway. Nick liked her style. It was obvious she had real talent. All the furniture was still in place. The house looked like the family was on a short vacation. Towels and linen were neatly stacked. Rachel's clothes were still hanging in the closet and in dresser drawers. Her perfume bottles and personal toilet notions were still in the bathroom. Her toothbrush was missing.

One guest bedroom looked like it was a playroom for Jonathan. It was across the hall from his bedroom upstairs. Nick looked closely and could just barely make out where a missing trunk, may have been placed. So far, he hadn't found a trunk, of any size, anywhere in the house. Nick was impressed how spotlessly clean the house was. No dust or musty smells. Nick guessed Maureen probably visited regularly, still waiting for Rachel to return. Probably had the maid come over to dust. Nick saved the basement and garage for last. It was apparent that Barry didn't have any woodworking hobbies that required power tools. A small, inexpensive work bench was placed against one wall in the garage. A serious handyman would have had at least a vise attached to the bench, none was there. A pegboard was fastened to the wall above the bench and held a few cheap tools; once again, nothing that would satisfy a true handyman.

A pair of fairly new men's work gloves occupied the shelf beneath the bench, along with a large bolt-cutter, the type used to break locks. For someone who didn't appear to be handy with tools, this looked out of place. Nick looked carefully around the garage and didn't spot any yard tools except for a long handled shovel and a leaf rake. The Ace Hardware label was still visible through a film of what appeared to be some sort of dust on the shovel. There was nothing else to suggest Barry had a green thumb. No mowing equipment, so Barry didn't cut the grass or work in the yard. So why then work gloves?

Rachel's Mercedes also had a film of dust covering it, yet the interior looked clean. Once again, no evidence that anyone had bothered to check for finger prints. From the appearance of the trunk, it had never been used, it looked like new. In the glove box, Nick found Rachel's cell phone. Why wouldn't she have taken that with her? Instead, she had to use a pay phone from New Orleans and call collect, making it easy to document her whereabouts. That one call also helped to eliminate Barry as a suspect, according to the sheriff's report.

Like her car, the batteries in the cell phone were dead. And why stop to buy just six gallons of gas, when it was obvious Rachel wasn't coming back anytime soon, since

Searching for Rachel

she'd purchased a one-way ticket? There was a paper trail leading to New Orleans, but something wasn't right, in Nick's opinion. The search for Rachel had essentially stopped in the Smithville area, once the investigation shifted to New Orleans. It reminded Nick of the way a quarterback, in a football game, would sometimes look to his right side, to throw off the defensive backs, then throw a pass to someone on the left side.

Chapter 6

Barry Greene sat on one of four high stools at a small round table in the middle section of the Harry's bar, now his favorite, and recently discovered, watering hole on the square in downtown Ocala. The small round tables were clustered close together, affording easy conversation during happy hour. It was early and the weather channel was indicating a storm moving across Florida later in the evening. From his lofted position, Barry could easily scan the booths lining the outer wall. Sitting in the middle of the room gave him high visibility. He knew that in another fifteen minutes the place would be filled. And to his surprise, on his last visit, a lot of good-looking younger women patronized Harry's. It looked like an upscale singles bar. Quite a few of the patrons seemed to know others in the room.

Over time Barry hoped that his presence would be noticed. And perhaps some available younger woman would give him a subtle signal that she might be interested in getting together. He liked an aggressive woman in the sack. Usually they were independent and had a decent job, or owned a business. This is where that crowd hung out, and where he decided to do his trolling. He was through fooling around with waitresses and receptionists. He

Searching for Rachel

wanted a classy lady who smelled good and wore expensive, sexy underwear.

In the past five months Barry had checked out most of the bars in and around Ocala. He liked the country club, but most of the available women there were older. It was members only and Barry used the company's account number. Part of his sales approach to hot prospects was to take them to the country club for lunch after viewing several homes in the area. It was an easy way to recap what had been shown, find out what they liked, and to close in on how much house they could afford. It helped a lot if they were golfers, or played tennis.

Barry had been aware of Ocala's popularity ever since he began selling real estate. Some of his former clients had sold their homes in Tennessee and had moved there. So he used the Internet and began some research on the area just a few weeks before Ezra dropped the bomb on him, telling the world, on TV, that he thought his son-in-law was somehow responsible for his daughter's disappearance. The old bastard had no proof to support his insinuation and Barry seriously considered suing him for slander. The problem was, no local attorney would consider representing him. They were all afraid of Ezra's power and influence. Two different lawyers told him, he didn't stand a chance going up against Ezra.

Ocala had been a smart move. Barry had real estate experience, and if all else failed, he could always get a job selling cars and trucks again. He'd been fortunate to land a job selling real estate almost immediately. He'd also been fortunate to find a nice, furnished two-bedroom condo to lease for a year. And not too far away from the condo, he found a sweet older lady willing to watch Jonathan after school, and on weekends, when he had to work. Yes, things were falling into place, he thought. He was aware that his son missed his grandparents, and his dog. There was a little satisfaction knowing Ezra and Maureen missed the boy, too. Ezra should have thought things through before shooting off his big mouth.

"Hello there, would you mind if we shared this table with you, or are you waiting for someone?" There were two ladies standing beside him. The one talking to him had caught him momentarily thinking about Ezra. Both appeared to be in their late twenties, thirty maybe. Nicely dressed and attractive. His plan, to drink at Harry's, was definitely working.

"Please join me. You caught me when I was six hundred miles away."

"Six hundred miles in which direction?" The blond asked. Both sat opposite him.

"Nashville area. That's where I'm from. Name's Barry by the way."

"Well hi again. I'm Amanda and this is Judy. I think we've seen you in here before haven't we?"

"Probably. I stop in after work for a quick drink and to catch the news," Barry said casually. There was an art to trolling and it was never a good idea to act too fast with classy ladies.

"I hardly ever watch the news anymore, it's too depressing. So what kind of work do you do, Barry?" Amanda asked. Judy held up her hand to signal the waitress.

"I sell real estate. How 'bout you?"

"I'm a travel consultant. If you ever decide to take a cruise somewhere, give me a call." Amanda opened an expensive-looking purse, searched for a card case and gave Barry her card. It was the card she used, whenever she met someone new, someone she didn't really know.

"And she's good, too," Judy added. Barry wasn't sure she was in the conversation until she spoke. Judy wasn't the hot number, it was her friend, Amanda who was giving

Searching for Rachel

off all the right signals. Barry liked everything about her. He was being careful to maintain eye contact, not stare below her neck, at her ample bust. Some women liked to be ogled, the ones who wore cheap perfume, cheap gaudy jewelry, chewed gum and winked, hoping someone would buy them a drink. Barry'd been there, done that and regretted the final outcome whenever he'd taken the bait. Harry's didn't cater to that type crowd, confirming his earlier decision to stake his claim here.

"In that case, here's my card. And if you're ever interested in buying some investment property, give me a call."

"Don't you handle other type listings as well?"

"Sure, but you ladies look like you're pretty well-established already."

"I guess you mean that as some sort of compliment," Amanda said.

"Actually no. It was more a statement of fact. You both look like professional business women. What do you do, Judy?" Barry was thinking about another Gin and Tonic and decided against it.

"I manage a discount book store. I don't own it, so I don't think of myself as a professional or anything like that."

"I guess if we boil it all down to the basics, I'd say the three of us are all in sales, in one form or another. That's not something to ever be ashamed of," Barry said. "I know I'm not."

"I agree," Amanda said. Her friend nodded.

"I'm not ashamed of what I do, I just thought you might think I owned the business, but I don't,"Judy added. It was an unnecessary qualification.

"I'll let you ladies have the table, I've got to get going." Barry finished his drink, picked up his check and walked to the bar to pay his bill.

After paying, he returned to the table, left a five-dollar tip and said, "Nice talking to you both. Maybe I'll see you in here again." He waved and walked out. There was a time when he would have offered to buy their drinks, hoping to get lucky later. He knew that to be a foolish approach here. Better to let them come onto him, the next time he was there. He reminded himself that he should never look like a guy eager to get laid, even though he was. He was also being careful.

Barry stopped at a fast food place for some take-out on his way over to Mrs. Pearlman's house to get Jonathan. Mrs. Pearlman was a widow who lived alone with her small Terrier. It was a good substitute for Jake.

Pulling into the condo complex, Barry had to park several spots farther away than normal because of the late hour. It still annoyed him that he had to park his Ford Explorer outside, leaving it exposed to the elements. Jonathan was busy telling him about his day and asking if he could go to the pool later. Barry only caught part of it because he was thinking about Amanda. She was the aggressive one. Her friend, Judy was a little on the shy side by comparison.

He wondered if they discussed him after he left. Maybe think he was a seven, a ten being reserved for the hunks who flashed tans and muscle, who had tight asses, perfect white teeth, and were probably gay, he mused. Judy reminded him of some of the secretaries he'd dated. She dressed well enough, but didn't have the class that Amanda had. Amanda radiated a sexual energy that excited him. She would be a challenge for anyone. Amanda wore a skirt and showed off her shapely legs while her friend, Judy wore slacks. Her legs might also be shapely, but it would take longer to find out. He'd learned that the fast crowd flashed their assets. Hidden qualities took time to be revealed.

Searching for Rachel

Barry clicked the lock button on his key ring and walked toward the front entrance to the condo. Jonathan carried the take-out. His unit was on the second floor with a view of the parking lot. Being somewhat absorbed with Amanda, Barry was unaware of the man sitting in a black Ford Taurus in the next parking section.

Gordon worked for Charles McBride. And Charles McBride's private investigative agency was currently working for Ezra Rueben. Gordon noted the time of Barry's arrival, phoned it into the office and waited for thirty more minutes, just in case Barry decided to go out again, which he sometimes did. It was doubtful tonight since he had the kid with him. Gordon sat outside Harry's and watched Barry order a drink. Barry was becoming predictable and it was easy to anticipate where he was going after work. During the day, during working hours, Gordon didn't bother with following Barry around. They knew where he worked and so far he hadn't done anything unusual. They also had an illegal tap on his home phone and nothing proved interesting there, either.

"Okay, I'm pulling the plug for tonight guys. The subject is tucked in and watching television, which I'm about to do when I get home," Gordon said to himself, noting the time on his clipboard. Gordon had a transponder fastened to the rear section of the Explorer's frame, just in case he ever lost Barry in heavy traffic. With Gordon's help, McBride knew where Barry was every hour of every day and reported this to Ezra at least once a week ever since Barry arrived. For Gordon, it had become a boring assignment. He was hoping Barry would get lucky soon, just to watch the guy getting some action. He'd been cruising all the pubs the last few months, even slowed down a few times, to check out a few working street girls, but never stopped. So far, he was behaving, much to Gordon's chagrin.

After dinner, Barry turned on the television to entertain Jonathan while he examined the business card he'd been given earlier. Her name was Amanda McBride and her title said: Travel Consultant. She used a post office box for an address along with an email address. Only a cell phone was listed. Barry thought it was a strange card for someone who dealt with the public. It was like a temporary shield, he thought. Barry was also using a post office box for his mail, to keep his exact location a secret. Ezra would no doubt try to keep him on his personal radar screen and Barry was doing his best to avoid it.

Barry picked up the scrapbook he'd been keeping with all the newspaper items about Rachel's disappearance. The event had been well-documented in the Nashville and Smithville newspapers. The most recent clipping was of Ezra's reward offer. Barry could just imagine how that sat with Sheriff Bobby Joe. Until Rachel's disappearance, Barry had never met the sheriff, or had any dealings with his office. In his opinion, the sheriff was sort of a laid back kind of guy who looked directly at you, half expecting you to spill your guts about whatever he was questioning you about. He nodded his head a lot and would look away, like he was considering what you just told him. It was hard to read him, you didn't know if he believed you, or not. Every time they talked, he made Barry feel slightly uncomfortable. Ezra was no doubt pushing him from behind the scenes, and planting ideas. Still, the sheriff had been decent toward him. Maybe he even felt a little sympathy, Barry wondered.

Between some empty pages a photo slipped out. It was their wedding picture, the one he used to have framed, sitting on his desk soon after he started working for Ezra.

Searching for Rachel

Not only were they an attractive couple, but the photo was like a big neon sign, telling all those who worked in the office, *this was the boss's son-in-law, beware.* It was like a page torn from a psychology book he'd once read. It was a way to gain instant respect, because everyone feared Ezra. Everyone, except Barry. Their relationship was one of mutual annoyance and suspicion. Ezra probably checked Barry's waste basket after he left work, Barry thought.

Barry could still remember the first time he met Rachel. She was recently out of college, spoiled and sexy. She had a great tan having just recently returned from six months playing around in France and Spain. Daddy had agreed to buy her a new sports car and Barry wanted to be the one who sold it. He found out everything about her, using a credit application form, even though it wasn't necessary, since it was a cash deal. And later, he'd personally delivered the Beamer to her parent's home in Smithville. He wanted to see where she and her parents lived. Barry had his friend, Keith follow him so he had a ride back. He'd left the top down with a single red rose and a brief note on the driver's seat. Barry tried to remember what the note said. Something like, *If you ever need anything, just give me a call* and signed it, *Barry.*

Later, Barry learned that Ezra had actually bought the car for her 23rd birthday. It was a silver BMW convertible with a black leather interior. It was a beautiful car meant to be driven by a beautiful new owner. He'd mentioned something to that effect while she was still in the showroom. He had tried not to come onto her that day. Keith said he was acting a little goofy. Knowing Keith, he was just jealous and envious.

Barry didn't know who Ezra Rueben was, then. He had to do some fast research to learn something about the real estate tycoon. What he'd learned was the man was rich. Ezra's name was on the check Rachel used to pay for the car.

Thinking back, Barry remembered it was three days after he delivered the car, when he sent her a thank you note along with two dozen long stem red roses. When she called to thank him, he asked her out, promising to personally take care of all her automobile maintenance for as long as she owned the car, and dated him. Later, she told him she thought his approach was quite an original pick-up line. She also thought he was cute, even though he was about ten years older. While in Europe, she told him she'd dated a few older men and decided they had more maturity. Over the next few months of dating, Barry and Rachel discovered they had a few differences other than age. She liked Rock music, he didn't. She liked red wine, Barry drank Coors Lite. She played tennis, he played golf. In bed, those differences evaporated.

After two months of dating, Barry decided the only way he'd ever gain any favor with Ezra was to learn as much as possible about real estate. He enrolled in a night school course, took a job with a small real estate firm in Nashville, and eventually earned his license. It was enough to impress Ezra, he thought. He knew that in time, Ezra would learn more about Barry and find out that he didn't come from a prominent Jewish family. He hoped his ambitious nature would count for something. And apparently it did. Ezra hired him and monitored his progress. Barry had surprised everyone, quickly reaching or exceeding the goals he'd been given. Barry knew that Ezra still had reservations about him. It was Maureen who had helped sway Ezra when he and Rachel became engaged. Barry learned that Maureen wanted to become a grandmother.

Later, Barry found out from Maureen that it had been Ezra's greatest wish to have a grandson, although he never mentioned it. Ezra got that wish two years after he and Rachel were married. It had taken some ingenuity to get Rachel pregnant, because she wanted to wait to have children. That was five years ago, Barry recalled, closing the scrapbook. A lot had happened in the past seven years since he'd met Rachel. It had been the red hair and independent attitude that had first attracted him. Now that he thought about it, Amanda McBride seemed to also have an independent manner. She was closer to a strawberry blond. And she certainly looked like she worked out regularly. He was looking forward to seeing her again, maybe ask her about a cruise, and if she'd go with him, as a personal guide. It gave him something new to think about.

Richard Standring

Chapter 7

Nick Alexander used his vast resources to do a background check on Barry Greene as well as Ezra Rueben. Nick subscribed to a special data base that allowed him to access a wide variety of information. Neither had any criminal records and both were who they claimed to be, no aliases. Barry had a service record with an honorable discharge. Neither had a bankruptcy in the past, nor one pending. Ezra's estimated wealth was far greater than Nick had anticipated. Nick decided to check in at the real estate office in Smithville, hoping that Ezra wouldn't be there. He wanted to pick up on some local gossip. In small towns, everyone seemed to know a little, or a lot about what was going on. Nick was certain the sheriff was plugged into all of it.

While Nick had been busy checking out Barry and Ezra, Deputy Randy Cooper was busy checking on Nick's background. As his business card indicated, he was currently a private investigator in Saint Clair Shores, an eastern suburb of Detroit. Nick had retired from the Saint Clair Shores Police Department as a lieutenant in charge of detectives and homicides with an excellent record. He was divorced with one son who was out of college and working for a law firm in Detroit.

Searching for Rachel

"He has an impressive client list by the way," The captain said on the phone. "And the reason you wanted all this again?"

"Like I said, some rich fellow fella here in Smithville has apparently asked him to look into his daughter's disappearance. Naturally when some one presents his business card saying he's a pee eye, we want to check him out, make sure he's the real deal, know what I'm sayin'?" the deputy had been scribbling notes as he talked to one of Nick's former associates.

"I'll tell you this much, Nick's as thorough as any detective I've ever known. He's closed his fair of tough cases here. Cut him some slack, he likes to work alone, but he gets results."

"Not much help I can give him right now. It's a cold case, getting colder every day she's not found."

Deputy Randy re-wrote his notes into something more legible and put the report on the sheriff's desk. Despite the glowing commentary, Randy had reservations. This wasn't Detroit, this was the sticks. People were a lot different here. They didn't open up to strangers, particularly Yankee strangers, no siree. Mister Nick was going to be hard put to get too many straight answers. He'd been tempted to ask that captain he talked with how much a police lieutenant made a year up there. He was pretty damned sure it was a lot more than he was making, maybe even more than the sheriff.

Billy Ray Randall recognized Nick Alexander the minute the man walked into the real estate office. Billy Ray remembered Ezra walking over and taking Nick's business card out of his hand, when he heard Billy ask, "What brings a private investigator to Smithville". This time, Nick wasn't looking for Ezra. He was looking for the person

53

who picked up Barry at the Marina on the Monday after Rachel left. When Billy Ray heard the open question, he raised his hand, just like a kid still in school.

"That was me," Billy Ray said, offering to shake hands.

"Did Barry call you at the office that morning?" Nick asked.

"The phone was ringing when I opened the door."

"And you picked him up and brought him to the office?"

"Not exactly, I picked him up at the marina, but I dropped him off at his house, so he could get his Explorer," Billy Ray said.

"How long after that did he show up here?"

"Oh I guess it was about a half hour or so. You still looking at Barry as a suspect?"

"No, just trying to re-establish all the facts. After all, it's been almost seven months since Rachel disappeared."

"Yeah, it was a shock to everyone. Old Barry had to pack up and get out of Dodge, after Ezra threw him under the bus." Nick had heard that expression used before and knew it meant something similar to the expression, threw him to the wolves.

"When Barry showed up here at the office, was he wearing the same clothes as when you picked him up?"

"No, he'd changed. He had on shorts and sneakers when I picked him up. He had on a shirt and slacks when he came into the office. Nobody here is allowed to be too casual. Can't smoke in the office, either."

"Did Barry smoke?"

"I don't think so. I never saw him with a cigarette. It'd be stupid, Ezra hates smokers, can't stand to be around 'em."

"Ezra is a little difficult to work for, isn't he?"

Searching for Rachel

"Keep in mind he's the boss, okay? So I wouldn't want any of this to get back to him, or I'd get fired. But yeah, he can bust your balls. He's got his rules and everybody had better follow them, or you're out of here."

"I guess he was pretty hard on Barry."

"Oh yeah, you could say that. He was always giving Barry a hard time."

"Was Barry a good salesman?"

"Yes he was. He could read people. He could charm a snake."

"But he couldn't charm Ezra, could he?" Nick asked.

"No he couldn't. But then again, nobody could."

"Which desk was Barry's?"

"That one over there, but you won't find anything. Ezra cleaned it out the day after Barry left. Nobody here wants to use it. Bad luck."

"Anyone here been in touch with Barry since he left?"

"You gotta be kidding me, right? That would be like suicide."

"When Barry was still here, did he ever mention having any problems?"

"Only with Ezra. The old man and he had a few arguments about how to treat prospects, where to handle the closings, stuff like that. And, now that I think about it, the old man was pissed about Barry taking off on Wednesdays to play golf. He played golf with some of his buddies at the car dealership, where he used to work in Nashville."

"Any problems concerning Rachel?"

"Nothing. He had her picture, and his son's picture, on his desk. He was a real family man. Everybody here liked him."

Nick's next stop was in Nashville, to visit the car dealership where Barry worked, when he met Rachel. Nick wanted to get some sort of a picture of Barry before he entered real estate, before he became a married man.

"Anyone here remember Barry Greene when he worked here?" Nick asked.

"Sure. I'm still here, and I worked with the now famous Barry. Name's Keith Snyder. You looking to trade that Crown Vic?"

"I'm afraid not. Just looking for some information about Barry." Nick presented his card.

"I don't know what I could tell you. Barry worked here for several years, then he decided to go into real estate. While he was here he met a young rich girl he had the hots for and later, he married her. Barry married into some big time money."

"Are you aware his wife is missing?"

"Are you kidding me, the whole world knows she's missing. From what I hear, Barry is missing, too. So which one are you looking for?"

"Both maybe. I hear Barry is in Ocala and Rachel may be in New Orleans, but nobody seems to know where exactly."

"I can't help you out there, sorry."

Nick thought Keith was acting a little nervous. It was still late morning and there weren't any customers on the lot, or in the showroom.

"Can I buy you a cup of coffee?" Nick asked. He had a few more questions and didn't want Keith to walk away from him.

"The coffee here isn't all that good."

"Is there someplace close by where we could go?" Nick asked.

"Yeah, we could walk over to the Huddle House. We used to go over there all the time when Barry worked here."

They sat at the counter and waited for someone to take their order. Nick could smell the grease coming from the grill on the other side. He would have preferred a table, but most were occupied, the rest still had remains from a previous customer. They seemed to be short on help.

"This place has gone down hill. It used to be much nicer a few months ago. We'd eat lunch here just about every day. They had a few cute waitresses working here then. The ones working here now say moo in stead of hello." Keith laughed at his own attempt at humor.

"You don't eat here now?"

"Naw, I pack a sandwich and eat whenever we're not busy. Sometimes I don't get to eat until late in the afternoon."

"Sounds like a busy dealership."

"You bet. We sell a lot of product. You should give some thought to trading that Crown Vic while it's still worth something. How many miles you got on it?"

Ever the salesman, Nick thought. And typical. "I'll keep you in mind when the time comes. Tell me something, were you and Barry friends?"

"Yeah, sort of. Barry was a good car salesman, but not quite as good as I am. He made good money here."

"Were you one of the guys Barry played golf with on Wednesdays after he left?"

"What are you talking about? Nobody played any golf with Barry. He'd stop by and chew the rag with us for an hour, tell us about how he was doing, then buzz off. Probably had a little chickie stashed somewhere. Had to keep below the old man's radar."

"Did Barry fool around much when he worked here?"

"I guess I shouldn't answer that, because then you'd ask me how was it that I'd know that. Keep in mind, Barry was single when he worked here. Me, I'm married. When I get a day off, I cut the grass."

For Nick, that was as good as a yes. There was a time, after Nick was divorced, when he dated a lot of women:

Mostly secretaries, receptionists and a lot of waitresses. Waitresses seemed to have an instant thing for cops.

"I'll bet you get a fair number of single business women out shopping around for a Beamer don't you?"

"Oh yeah. That's why I don't wear my wedding ring when I'm working. Single chicks don't want to deal with some older married guy. Oops, you married?" Keith was suddenly aware that Nick was probably twenty years older than he was.

"Thinking about it," Nick replied, laughing to ease the moment.

"Did you ever meet, or see a picture of Rachel?" Nick pulled out the color photo Maureen had given him. He laid it on the counter, away from his coffee mug.

"Yeah, I saw her when she was in here buying that convertible Barry sold her, but she looks a lot better in this picture. She's a real looker." Keith picked up the photo and admired it.

The manager was standing by the register, close enough to catch part of their conversation. Now he walked over to refill their mugs. "Hey Keith, who's that? One of your new girlfriends?" It was obvious the man knew Keith as a regular customer.

"Remember Barry? Well this is his wife, Rachel," Keith said handing over the picture so the manager could take a better look.

"The one who's missing? No shit, this is her?" The manager took his time examining the photo with a good deal of interest. "You know who she reminds me of? Liz. You remember Liz when she worked here? You change the color of her hair to blond, and she could be Liz's twin sister."

"Of course I remember Liz. She was the only one we'd let wait on us when we used to eat here. Nice jugs, and not afraid to let you see 'em."

"I sure wish she still worked here. Business isn't the same since she left," the manager said.

"Why did she leave?" Nick asked.

"I've gotta get back to work," Keith said getting up.

"I may have a few more questions later," Nick said. He remained seated and kept the photo on the counter.

"It's funny. She was by far the best waitress we ever had here. She worked here about ten years. And like Keith said, she flirted with the guys. Married, single, young, old it didn't make any difference. She charmed them all and they loved it. That's what you do, if you want big tips, and those guys were big tippers, particularly that Barry. I think she had a thing for him."

"Did she ever date him?"

"Who knows? I try to keep my nose out, know what I mean?"

"So did something happen?"

"I guess so, but I can't tell you what it was. One day she just up and quit. Never even stopped back to pick up her check. I had to mail it to her."

"Really? How long ago was this?"

"Well it was last summer, end of July." *About the time Rachel disappeared*, Nick considered the coincidence.

"Do you still have her address and phone number?"

"Sure, but it won't do you any good. She's moved. When her check came back undelivered, I went over to her place, she was gone."

"That's very strange," Nick said.

"Tell me about it."

As soon as Keith was back at his desk, he picked up the phone and called Barry's cell phone number.

He got his message center. "Hey Barry, it's Keith. I got some bad news, old buddy. There was a private dick here today, asking a lot of questions about you."

Chapter 8

Barry Greene was at work when he retrieved Keith's brief message. It didn't surprise him. He knew Ezra would track him down wherever he went, and spend countless dollars keeping tabs on him. If someone was still checking on him in the Nashville area, even though he was no longer there, then Ezra probably had someone in Ocala doing the same thing. The thought put him in a sour mood. Jonathan planned to talk with his grandparents this coming weekend. He had to think of some unique diversion to keep that from happening. Using Jonathan's love for his grandparents, as a weapon of revenge, was a nasty thing to do, he knew, and felt slightly guilty thinking about it. Never the less, he'd come up with something to stick it to Ezra.

He called Keith back. Nashville was on Central time so there was an hour's difference. "Hey Keith, it's Barry. You busy?"

"Of course I'm busy, you asshole. Did you get my message?"

"Yeah, thanks. Tell me about this guy you talked to."

"His card says he's a private investigator. He's from someplace in Michigan. The old man must be desperate if he had to go that far to get someone to check on you. Doesn't say much for our local talent does it?"

Searching for Rachel

"Hmm. Where in Michigan?" Keith read everything on Nick's card to him. "Let me check the zip code. That should give us a better idea." Barry held for a minute before Keith was back. "Okay, here it is. Saint Clair Shores is in the Detroit area."

"Tell me everything he asked about, and what you told him."

"Hey Barry? You're beginning to sound a little paranoid. I don't recall all the exact words, but he was feeling me out on whether or not you ever chased any skirts."

"What'd you tell him?"

"I said, 'maybe, after all you were single back then'. And he wanted to know if you were any good as a car salesman. I told him you stunk and that's the reason you quit."

"You did not. I was always ahead of you in sales and you know it."

"Oh, and we had a cup of coffee over at your old stomping grounds, where Liz used to work. Did you know she quit?"

"Uh no, I guess I didn't know that. Where'd she go?"

"For a while there I thought maybe you had her stashed someplace. She isn't down there in Ocala with you by any chance, is she?"

"Get real. She flirted with everyone and you know it."

"Yeah, but she had a thing for you. We figured you were getting some of that. I admit I tried once, but she turned me down." That wasn't entirely true, but Keith wasn't about to share everything with Barry.

"Well I never got any either. So where is she now?"

"Beats me. I heard the manager tell this Nick fella that she left suddenly. She never stopped back to pick up her paycheck."

"What the hell was this guy doing discussing Liz? I thought you said he was checking on me."

"Yeah, well he was showing Rachel's picture around see, and the manager comes over and says something about her looking a lot like Liz, only the color of her hair was different. You know what? She does look a lot like Liz, now that I've seen Rachel's picture."

"Really? I guess I never made that connection. I was too busy looking down the front of Liz's uniform to notice anything else."

"Well you weren't the only one, sport. Somebody must have come along and swept her off her feet. My guess is, it was one of those wannabe country musicians we see around here all the time. Gonna be a big star someday."

"Did you tell that to this investigator?"

"Nope. Let him figure it out for himself. I'm only interested in selling cars."

"Yeah, and getting laid."

"There's that, too. You getting any down there?"

"Been too busy." Keith wasn't buying that. He knew Barry well enough to know the guy always knew where the action was.

"If you need to call me, continue to use my cell phone number. I'm not sure if my home phone is secure," Barry cautioned.

"Barry my friend, you are definitely getting paranoid. If I run into Liz, should I give her this number?"

"That's the last thing you'd ever do and you know it." He and Keith had always been friendly rivals at the dealership. When they went out for drinks together after work, Keith was always the one who struck out, being too bold. After a few beers, he'd become vulgar, asking women he didn't even know, if they put out, and if so, would they like to have a drink with him. Sometimes he even embarrassed Barry, who would immediately apologize for

Searching for Rachel

his friend's bad behavior. Later, he'd return to buy them another drink, after Keith was gone. It could have become a good comedy routine. Keith opening the door and Barry playing Mr. Smooth, closing the deal. Sort of like the good cop, bad cop scenarios one saw on television.

The Liz link bothered him. He'd taken precautions so that no one would ever know about the two of them being together. At the Huddle House, she treated him just like she did all her other regular customers. No hint there was anything else going on between them. Liz flirted with all the men, young and old.

Liz had told him all about how she'd left Baton Rouge, Louisiana when she was just sixteen, and later changed her name from Lucille Fontaine to Liz Miller. She wanted something simple that people could remember. She'd lived with a cousin in Memphis for a while and learned to become a waitress. Later, she became a street prostitute after her cousin threw her out. Her cousin's boyfriend was a truck driver and came onto her one night when he was drunk. Her cousin caught the two of them together and blamed her.

Barry was surprised that she even admitted all that to him. She said she got tired of working the streets, as a cheap whore, getting beat up occasionally, and eventually took a job at the Huddle House, where she could be respectable and find someone nice to date, and maybe take care of her.

Barry was pretty sure that meant him. He'd dated Liz a few times while working at the dealership. He couldn't afford to be her sugar daddy, even though he was sure that was what she was looking for. He stopped seeing her for about a year. Later, he started seeing her again, on Wednesdays, after he was married to Rachel. He made sure no one knew about it, not even Keith. Barry used the excuse; he was playing golf, in Nashville, with some of his old car buddies on Wednesdays, when he was really shacking up with Liz. She took off a half-day on Wednesdays to accommodate him. He rarely took her anywhere. He couldn't afford to be recognized with her. If Ezra ever found out, Barry knew his future would be over. So he kept the affair to just Wednesdays, knowing that Liz was probably seeing other guys as well. She had hinted that there were others. She also made more tips than any of the other waitresses, something she was proud of. She used her sexuality to advantage, just like Marilyn Monroe did.

Liz could do a great Marilyn Monroe impersonation, wiggling her cute behind at him and blowing him a kiss from those bright red lips of hers while bending over in a pose, giving him a great view. She knew more ways to satisfy him than any other woman he'd ever known.

To help compensate her, Barry had given her the down payment on a used car, a Honda Civic, he'd taken in on trade, soon after they started dating. Eventually, he made most of the payments. She never asked him for money, just hinted that she was having a hard time making ends meet. Barry often wondered if she charged any of the others she was seeing. Over time she became a good escape from the hectic life he experienced in Smithville despite the risk.

Barry could still remember the nightmare he'd had about a year ago. In his dream, Liz had mentioned that she was pregnant and he was the father. She agreed to get an abortion, but he had to pay all the expenses, including the time she had to take off work to recover. It was a vivid dream. Even though Barry always used protection, and Liz she was on the pill, it was still a scary dream. What if she got pregnant by someone else she was seeing and blamed him? It had the potential for blackmail, something he worried about after he was married. If Rachel, or Ezra, ever found out, it could be the end of everything.

Searching for Rachel

Well, he really wasn't concerned about Liz anymore. She was out of his life and no longer a threat, unless someone discovered his past relationship with her. If questioned, he planned to say that he used to see her while he worked at the car dealership and broke it off once he became engaged to Rachel, which was partially true.

Barry thought it interesting that his friend, Keith had even suggested that maybe Liz was down in Ocala with him. Was he fishing? He hoped Keith hadn't mentioned something like that to this Nick character. Ezra would love to get something on him that might allow Ezra and Maureen to get custody of Jonathan. That wasn't going to happen.

From now on, he had to be doubly careful. He'd escaped Ezra's local influence, but the man was able to hire people anywhere, even Michigan.

Barry decided to start using the computers at the local library for his email messages rather than to use his laptop at home. He wasn't sure if his computer at work was entirely safe, either. And if his work computer was being monitored, why not his work phone as well? Yes, he had to be extremely careful.

It occurred to him that Ezra might even go so far as to hire someone to snatch Jonathan. Barry knew Ezra wasn't beyond doing something illegal if it benefited him. He'd uncovered a few details of some shady deals.

Barry liked Ocala and wished he'd made the move several years sooner. Of course Rachel would never even consider leaving Smithville and being near her parents. To move somewhere else again now, would be too big of a disruption. He'd have to find a new school for Jonathan, a new baby sitter and another job. It was just too much of a hassle to even contemplate leaving Ocala. If only Ezra would die of a heart attack or something, then his worries would end. He knew Maureen wouldn't pursue him. She just went along with Ezra, and whatever he wanted to do. So why wasn't Rachel more like her mother, he asked himself again. It was because of Ezra's influence. He dominated the entire family, the bastard! The way Barry viewed it, directly, or indirectly, Ezra was the real source of all his problems.

Chapter 9

Ezra Rueben called Nick at Carol's house while they were eating breakfast. Nick's smile disappeared as soon as he heard Ezra's voice.

"I thought I'd hear something from you by now," Ezra said, without any formalities.

"I'm still gathering information and have a few more people to talk to before I make a trip down to Ocala."

"Ocala is a waste of time. I already have someone there keeping an eye on Barry. I get regular reports on what he's doing, where he's been and who he sees. That's more than I'm getting from you."

Nick ignored the jab. "Rueben, you'll have to be patient. I know that may be difficult for you, but I have my own way of working a case and this one will take some time."

"What have you found out so far?" Ezra asked, cutting him short.

"Why don't I give you a report the end of the week instead of bits and pieces," Nick said trying to hide his annoyance.

"Maureen tells me you checked out the house. Find anything of interest there?"

"Sometimes it's what you don't find. There's no evidence that anything has been disturbed. I'm not sure how thorough the sheriff's people were in checking the area."

"You'd have to define thorough. I'm not convinced they did a very good job of checking anything. It was a spotty effort to appease me. Maureen was the one who discovered one of the suitcases and a few clothes missing. Apparently Rachel stopped back at the house before leaving for the airport."

"Well that makes sense. I've been checking into Barry's background …."

Again, Ezra cut him short, "I've already had someone do that. There's nothing there worth pursuing. I know all there is to know about Barry Greene and it doesn't even fill a page worth reading."

"Make sure I see a copy of what you have. I should have seen it before I made a trip over to Nashville yesterday."

"If you'd checked in with me first, I'd have given it to you." Click. Ezra had hung up with saying goodbye. Abrupt and rude, Nick thought. Throw in arrogant as well. This was definitely going to be a difficult assignment, just as the sheriff had hinted.

"So did that help get your heart started?" Carol asked. She was about to leave for work.

"I think Mr. Rueben is used to having things go his way, regardless of the rules." Nick wasn't sure how much he wanted to reveal to his client at this stage. What he had so far was mostly speculation.

Nick called Ezra's home number and Maureen answered.

"Ezra left early to do some things in the office. You might be able to reach him in Nashville." She gave Nick the number.

"Thanks, Mrs. Rueben,"
"Please call me Maureen."
At least one member of the family was civil and displayed manners. Nick could see why Barry played to her rather than Ezra. An hour and a half later, Nick walked into Ezra's posh Belle Mead office and found him talking with his secretary, at her desk. Ezra spotted Nick and motioned for him to follow into his private office.
"Well?" Ezra didn't waste words.
"I won't take up much of your time, Ezra," Nick decided it was time to be more informal and call the man by his first name. "you cut me a little short on the phone earlier. I wanted to tell you, that in addition to making a trip to Ocala, I also think a trip to New Orleans is in order."
"And what do you think you'll accomplish there? "
"I guess I won't be able to answer that until I've made the trip."
"You may as well know I hired an investigator down there to do some independent looking around, but he didn't find anything of interest. His name is Herschel Fielding and he came highly recommended. He told me he double-checked the hospitals, the morgue and all the local hotels and motels, even a few out-of-the-way places like bed and breakfast establishments that the police might have overlooked. He was quite thorough. He even checked some of the homeless shelters, although I can't see Rachel living like that. I think if she was down there, he would have found her."
"Give me his address and phone number and I'll check in with him when I'm there," Nick said. "And you might as well give me Barry's new address and whatever you have since he moved to Ocala. You mentioned that you have someone watching him down there, I'll check in with them as well." Nick didn't like it that Ezra saw fit to feed him bits of information at a time.

"For what this is costing me, I expect some results and some reports on anything you feel is unusual. Anything, you understand?"

"Oh yes, I fully understand." Nick felt it wasn't a good time to get into an argument. He just wanted Ezra to know that despite warnings, that he was wasting time, Nick planned to make both trips, if he was to continue the investigation.

"By the way, has anyone attempted to collect the reward yet?"

"No, and that sort of surprises me. Do you think I should increase the amount?"

"No. I wouldn't do that. If anyone knows anything important, they should have come forward by now. I'll have to do some back tracking and that's going to take some time. So, don't be impatient if I don't have something to report right away. This is a cold case with only a few leads. I want to talk to everyone the police interviewed." *And maybe a few the police didn't even know about,* Nick said to himself.

Nick wondered if Carol had ever been to New Orleans? If not, maybe she could get away for a few days and go with him.

Searching for Rachel

Chapter 10

Liz Miller lived in an older apartment building on the north side of town, in a mixed neighborhood that was beginning to show signs of decay. It reminded Nick of sections of Detroit. People had to leave their vehicles parked on the street, exposed to vandalism. People sat on porch steps watching the passing scene. They knew when a strange car arrived. Like Detroit, they could spot an unmarked as soon as it appeared. Nick's Crown Vic looked like an unmarked police car. Several teenagers took off running as soon as Nick parked the car. He found the superintendent in the rear of the building in the hallway of a downstairs apartment.

"She lived here about eight years. Had a few gentleman friends I guess. Never was any trouble. She always paid her rent on time. Then suddenly she's gone. Left all her furniture and junk and stuck me for a month's rent."

"Ever see this man with her?" Nick showed a photo of Barry that he'd taken from the house.

"Yeah, he came around regularly. Usually it was a Wednesday I seem to recall. Don't ask me his name 'cause I don't make it my business to know. This ain't exactly the

Ritz, ya know. You pay your rent, you're entitled to some privacy. That's the way I figure it."

"What did you do with the furniture Liz Miller left?"

"Hey it was all junk. Gave it to the Goodwill."

Sure you did. Nick didn't buy any of that, but at least he now knew that Liz definitely left suddenly for some unknown reason. Perhaps Barry could shed some light on that. Two women who looked a lot alike were now missing. Both went missing about the same time. And, both had a relationship with Barry. What were the odds of that happening? At least he knew a bit more about Barry and how he spent part of his Wednesdays. It was just a stroke of luck that he'd discovered the Liz connection. He doubted the sheriff, or Ezra knew anything about it.

"What kind of car did Liz drive?"

"She had an older model Honda. I think it was a Civic. Hard to tell what year some of those Jap cars are, they all look the same to me. It was a faded blue and the side view mirror was broken off, on the passenger side. That's the best I can do."

"Actually, that's a pretty good description. Thanks."

Driving back toward Smithville, Nick let his imagination run wild and loose, as it sometimes did, when he was driving a long stretch. He played his old game of *what if.* Everyone assumed that it was Rachel who left the houseboat that Sunday, and flew to New Orleans. What if it wasn't Rachel? Could it have been Liz Miller instead, spending the weekend with Barry? If she wore a wig, or dyed her hair red, she could easily pass for Rachel from a distance, particularly with big sunglasses. It was a wild what if, yet it presented a different scenario to consider.

And, if that was what happened, then Rachel could have disappeared sometime earlier, perhaps on Friday, or Saturday. Was her body stuffed in a trunk and dumped in the lake somewhere? Did Barry conveniently dump the missing trunk over the side, after it was dark? So far, Nick had a missing trunk and two missing women. Both were involved with Barry and both disappeared about the same time. If Nick could find Liz, perhaps some of these unanswered questions could be satisfied and Nick could begin to connect the dots. It was his favorite expression. And, was Barry still keeping in touch with Liz? Could she also be living in Ocala? For now, it was all pure speculation. But it also made sense. It was Nick's way of thinking outside the box.

Only this time the box happened to be a missing trunk.

While still driving, Nick thought about New Orleans. It was a romantic city and it could also be a dangerous city, depending on what you wanted, and how you went about getting it. Dixieland jazz was some of Nick's favorite music. His memory bank was already reviewing past places where he'd enjoyed wonderful meals. Unfortunately, time wouldn't permit hitting all of them.

Meanwhile, Rachel's husband was doing his waiting, if in fact he was waiting, in Ocala, Florida, supposedly away from his in-laws and their strong influence. The picture Nick saw in his mind was definitely out of sync with what logic would suggest. The worried husband should remain ever vigilant, and should remain at their home, expecting that the wife might soon return, He'd be there waiting, not in some distant city, where she might not find him.

So far, Nick had to agree with the sheriff, there didn't seem to be an apparent motive for Barry to harm his wife, or cause her to leave. There had to be a strong reason however, for her to leave the way she had. It appeared to be impulsive. Had Rachel found out about Barry and Liz? Was it possible she was the one fooling around? Had Ezra found out and sent her away? Or, was it possible that she was actually running away from her domineering father, not Barry? And why did she pick New Orleans as her destination? Then again, was it her final destination, or was it somewhere else close by like Baton Rouge or Biloxi? Nick doubted the search expanded beyond New Orleans. The dead end seemed to stop there, but not the questions.

Nick continued to allow his mind to wander. He thought about the basement of Barry and Rachel's house. Most basements and garages had some clutter, theirs was unusually neat. And what would Barry ever use a large bolt cutter on, other than a lock? He'd have to pursue that more when he returned from New Orleans.

Nick stopped by the sheriff's office on his way back to Cookeville. It was only a little out of the way. He wanted to know what else the sheriff might know about Barry, and at the same time, share his discovery about the missing trunk. He wanted the sheriff to think he was cooperating.

"Sheriff's not in right now, can I hep you with something?" Deputy Randy Stevens said, standing behind the counter, looking in-charge.

"Well maybe you can, deputy." Nick wondered why it was he kept running into Deputy Stevens. He seemed to be around all the time. "Tell the sheriff I stopped by and that there seems to be a trunk missing from the houseboat. They used it to store blankets, but the blankets are currently sitting on the floor in a closet. And Mrs. Rueben doesn't have any idea where it could be. She bought it for her grandson, to store his toys. Later it was moved to the houseboat." Listening to himself talk, Nick felt the report sounded a bit foolish.

"Did you check the house? Maybe it's back there."

"Yes, I checked, and it isn't there."

"So maybe it got sold at a yard sale or something. I can't see anyone stealing a trunk." By the smirk on his face, Nick could see the deputy thought this was funny.

"I don't think Mrs. Rueben or any of the family would get involved in yard sales, do you?"

"You can't never tell about rich folks. They can sure do some strange things. You got anything else you want me to pass on?"

"No, but let me ask you about Barry. Did he ever hang out with anyone, you know stop for drinks after work somewhere, anything like that?"

"I do all my hanging out at Gus's place south of town and I ain't never once saw him in there. And Gus has never mentioned it. If Barry had been in there, Gus sure would have told me about it, I guarandamntee ya. Fact is, not much goes on around these parts that the sheriff, or me, doesn't hear about it."

"I had a feeling that was the case. That's why I asked. So you don't think Barry was fooling around, seeing someone on the side maybe?"

"That'd be stupid. His wife was sure pretty enough and by now you've gathered there's a bit of money in the family. If he did any fooling around, he did it somewhere outside Smithville, where Mr. Rueben wouldn't catch him."

"I get the impression Ezra kept a close eye on Barry," Nick said.

"So I've heard. Now if it had been Barry that disappeared, we'd sure be taking a close look at the old man, yes sir. Not much love between 'em."

"It's funny, from all I've been able to learn so far, Barry appears to have been a good salesman. Ezra would benefit from his sales efforts."

"The way I see it, Ezra didn't ever need Barry, even if he was a good salesman. He used to sell cars, what does that tell you? Meets a rich girl and marries into the family thinkin' he's gonna hit pay dirt one day, when the old man goes toes up. Only it ain't happened yet. Probably not any time soon, either."

Nick thought that was a pretty fair evaluation of the situation. He'd made a similar conclusion earlier.

"I'll tell you what, Barry might be down there in Ocala, but you can bet the old man knows every move he's making. It was me, I'd go to Mexico," Randy said.

"I'm not sure that would be far enough away, but I agree with you," Nick said.

He'd put in an appearance with the sheriff's office, gave the impression he was cooperating, and learned where the deputy hung out when he was off duty. That could prove helpful later, if he wanted to engage the man in some more casual conversation. The trick was to make him feel important, like today. While in Smithville, Nick had one more stop to make.

Meredith Mayfield said she spoke with her best friend, Rachel just about every day. She told Nick they were roommates at Vanderbilt. When Rachel and Barry got married, she was the bridesmaid. She and Rachel talked about everything going on in their respective lives. Meredith's name and phone number was at the top of the list Maureen gave Nick.

"When was the last time you spoke with Rachel?" Nick asked.

"Let's see, it had to be Friday afternoon. I think it was around three o'clock. She was expecting Jonathan to be home soon, so we didn't yak too long."

"Uh huh, and did she mention that she was spending the weekend with Barry on the family houseboat?"

Searching for Rachel

"No, she never said anything about that. Actually I'm surprised, too. In fact, this is really weird, because Rachel mentioned that maybe we should get together sometime on Saturday to have some pizza and play cards. Why would she suggest that, if she and Barry were planning on being alone on the lake?"

"Maybe the houseboat weekend was Barry's last-minute idea and he hadn't sprung it on her yet," Nick said.

"Maybe, but she would have called me back. Sometimes we joined them. What really worries me is why she didn't call to say she was leaving for a few days. That's just not like her, you know? Rachel and I discuss everything, and I mean *everything*."

"And in discussing *everything*, how were things between Barry and Rachel? Were they having any problems?"

"Oh yeah. Barry and Ezra weren't getting along and she felt she was in the middle of their ongoing battle. No matter what Barry did at the office, it wasn't good enough for Ezra and he'd find fault. He seemed to delight in embarrassing Barry at work. You ask me, I'm surprised that Barry didn't just up and quit. He was a good enough to make it without Ezra."

"So Rachel understood the pressure on Barry?"

"Of course. But you have to realize, Rachel is still her daddy's little girl and she refused to take sides. It was making her a nervous wreck. Her folks were spoiling Jonathan like you wouldn't believe. That was a sore subject with Barry. And, she just found out that she was pregnant and she wasn't sure how Barry was going to take that news."

"She hadn't told him yet?"

"Not as of Friday afternoon, when we were on the phone together. She hadn't told anyone... except me."

"Were they trying to have another child?"

"Not really. I think it was an accident. In fact, Rachel commented once that Barry seemed to have lost interest in sex lately."

"Was it possible Rachel was seeing someone else?"

"Oh I doubt it. If she was, she never mentioned it to me. Are you suggesting that the baby wasn't Barry's?"

"No, I'm not suggesting anything, just exploring any and all reasons for her to disappear. Maybe she went to New Orleans to lose the baby rather than tell Barry about it. Maybe she didn't want him to know. Obviously it was early enough that he wouldn't notice," Nick said.

"Gee, I just don't know. I really don't think Rachel was having an affair with anyone, not that it never crossed her mind. She was attractive and kept in shape so she got a lot of looks when we'd be out together shopping."

"I can believe that. Was Barry the jealous type?"

"I think he considered Rachel more like a trophy- wife. He had what other guys could only dream about. He liked showing her off. No, I don't think he was really jealous. More like proud."

"Was there any hint that maybe Barry was fooling around?" Nick had to be careful not to suggest anything at this early stage. Speculation was always risky.

"Well if he was, and Rachel ever caught him, he'd be dead meat in a New York minute. The man would be a complete asshole to do anything like that. And with Ezra on his back, and looking over his shoulder, when would he ever have the time? The man was under a microscope."

"One more question. Rachel had a cell phone, right?"

"Of course. Everyone has a cell phone these days. She didn't go anywhere without it. Why?" *Because she went somewhere this time and didn't take it with her,* Nick thought.

"Well, knowing that, I'm surprised she didn't make some attempt to reach you, either before she left, or while on her way to the airport."

"That's why I think something happened to her. Maybe someone got into her car and took her credit cards and stuff. You read about these carjackers in the paper all the time. Maybe it was something like that."

"By the way, since you were a guest on the houseboat, do you recall seeing a trunk in one of the guest rooms?"

"Sure. They used it to store extra blankets. It used to be Jonathan's toy box when he was younger."

"Is it possible they might have sold it, or gotten rid of it?"

"I doubt it. It was a neat old trunk and very useful. I would have bought it, if they planned to get rid of it. Why, is it missing?"

"Not exactly, we just can't locate it."

"Oh. Do you think maybe, what I'm thinking?"

"I wouldn't go there just yet," Nick said. "And please, let's keep this whole conversation secret for now."

Nick left wondering if Barry knew that Rachel was pregnant? It was another question he'd ask, when he saw Barry in Ocala. What bothered Nick most was the fact that Rachel hadn't called her mother, or her best friend, both of whom she talked to just about every day. Other than Barry, Meredith may well have been one of the last people Rachel spoke with. And that was Friday afternoon around three o'clock. Sometime later, she must have taken her son to her parent's house. Nick made a mental note to ask Ezra what time she arrived, and was Barry with her? Nick also wondered if Ezra knew they were planning to use the houseboat that weekend? If not, perhaps the whole idea was spur of the moment, and not planned. And, why hadn't Rachel taken her cell phone with her?

Richard Standring

Chapter 11

Liz Miller had given Barry a brief outline of her earlier years, when she thought he really cared about her, wanted to know her better. When she first met Barry, he was single and looked like a good catch. She hesitated about giving him the full picture: About how she'd grown up in a poor family with three sisters and two brothers. Her mother took in laundry to help pay the bills and cleaned other people's houses. Her father was a part-time field hand and part-time drunk. They lived just outside Baton Rouge, Louisiana in a tar paper shack of a house with just two small bedrooms and an outhouse out back. Thinking back, it was hard to imagine growing up in such a confined arrangement.

When she was 15, Liz ran away from home. She'd lied and told Barry she was 16. She recalled being pregnant and scared. She couldn't reveal who the father was and knew her mother wouldn't believe that her favorite nephew, Leroy was the culprit. Leroy was 19 and had an old pickup truck, which he used to help Liz's mother deliver the laundry. Liz's mom thought the world of Leroy. The boy could do no wrong in her opinion. Liz was convinced her mom would never believe her, if she revealed the truth, so she didn't bother trying. It never

Searching for Rachel

occurred to her then, that maybe her mother actually suspected and was glad not to have a confrontation about it. Running away had solved the problem.

Leroy proudly revealed most of the secrets about sex to Liz when she was still 14. He drove her and her two younger brothers to a movie one Saturday afternoon in Baton Rouge. He was constantly trying to put his hand inside her dress to feel her up. Finally, after too many attempts, she stopped trying to resist. Her brothers were sitting in the front row while she and Leroy sat in the very last row of the darkened theatre. Leroy pointed to several other couples sitting close together and suggested they were engaged in similar fondling explorations. Later that same evening, Leroy came back by the house and sat on the front porch waiting for Liz to finish her chores in the kitchen. When she came out to sit on the porch, Leroy suggested they take a walk. Liz could still remember that evening as though it was yesterday.

Holding her hand, he talked about getting a job in the city, so he could make some money and buy a nice automobile. He promised he'd stop back and take her for a ride. Maybe stop for some ice cream. Liz already knew Leroy was a dreamer and a talker. That same evening he talked his way into her pants. It didn't take long after that one night of enlightenment for Liz to realize something was wrong when she became sick every morning. She wrote to her older sister, who lived in Memphis, and asked if she could come for a visit, never revealing her plan to escape. Her father had accused her of putting on weight and suggested that she eat less, not that there ever was much to eat with her two hungry brothers eating more than their share.

Liz left the dusty old shack, where she had lived for all her life, and walked away with a small sack of clothes and five dollars she'd managed to save. She told her mother she'd be back in a few weeks, knowing she'd never be back. Once she made it to the main highway a big truck stopped and gave her a lift as far as Vicksburg.

In return for the ride, she had to endure a brief sexual interlude of foreplay that developed into one more new sexual experience. Leroy had never asked her to perform oral sex. She found it repulsive, yet she survived the moment because she also knew it would soon be over, and she needed to get to Memphis, whatever the cost.

When you're poor, you must beg and do whatever others demand of you, she reasoned. She also vowed that her days of being poor would eventually end and she wouldn't have to beg, or take in other people's wash. And sex would be on her terms.

That experience was the beginning of a series of encounters she'd have with older men. She knew it was necessary to survive. Knowing how to satisfy older men also allowed her to manipulate them, and get what she wanted, which was freedom and independence. Later, she'd work on the security aspect.

Her second ride from Vicksburg into Memphis was another trucker and another similar episode. This time however, the driver offered her five dollars. She quickly realized that was as much money as her mother earned in a whole week washing clothes.

All she had to do was endure a few minutes of dirty talk and some temporary male dominance. Eventually she'd learn to turn all that to her advantage. Men were crude, vulgar creatures and very selfish, she quickly determined. She wondered how her mother had put up with her father for so many years. She also wondered if her father had made those same demands on her mother? It was a sordid thought that lingered all the way to Memphis. A woman had to be strong, and maybe a bit devious, to hold her own in the world, she thought as a way of

Searching for Rachel

justifying what she'd done. It was a lesson she'd come by the hard way, and not from her parents. It would, however, guide her future decisions.

By the time Liz arrived at her sister's trailer, just south of Memphis, near the Mississippi border, she had ten dollars and a lot more carnal knowledge. Before getting an abortion, and while in Memphis, she decided to change her name and selected Liz Miller. It was goodbye to Lucille Fontaine and a past she wanted to forget.

Liz's sister had worked as a waitress at a Waffle House, working the night shift, leaving Liz alone with her sister's boyfriend, Rodney. Rodney had a problem holding a steady job. Rodney also had a drinking problem. Liz quickly determined it was because he was lazy. As long as her sister supported him he wasn't motivated to get a job and help with the bills. In Liz's mind, men like that were worthless.

"Hey baby, why don't you come over here and sit with me so we can get better acquainted. I'll introduce you to some real bone," Rodney said the first morning Liz was alone with him.

"I ain't interested in your bone. I ain't interested in anything you got, which is nothing," she'd said.

"Oh yeah? You better watch that smart mouth of yours, girl. It could get you in a lot of trouble. 'Course you already in a bit of trouble from what I hear. Who's the daddy, or don't you know?"

"Just shut the hell up, Rodney. It's none of your damned business."

"Well I guess I don't see it that way. As long as you are staying under this roof, eatin' our food, you got no business bein' disrespectful. If I want somethin' from you, I can just take it, and you can't do nothin' 'bout it, you hear me?" As usual, he'd been drunk.

It didn't take Rodney long to start making moves on Liz. He would trap her in the small kitchen, after her sister left for work, force himself against her and fondle her. She hated the smell of his foul breath and cringed at his touch. He deliberately debased her with all the foul words he could think of. Some she'd never heard before.

She spent the first week locked in the spare bedroom, only going out after Rodney left for one of his local haunts. She felt like a prisoner in that small bedroom with one tiny window. She needed a plan to survive. She knew her sister couldn't help. She also knew it was impossible to avoid Rodney much longer, even when he was drunk.

She decided to let him think he was in control. Liz deliberately started to tease him, walking around in her underwear. She practiced and acquired a knowing smile, checking it in the bathroom mirror. The knowing smirk was complimented by a provocative way she began walking, swaying her rear end as if to say, "here it is, come and get it".

She knew all along what Rodney wanted. She also knew what she wanted. She'd already learned that men were willing to pay for sex, and she needed money to pay for an abortion. So if Rodney wanted to play, he would have to pay. She thought of how she'd trap him. Maybe leave the door ajar to her bedroom and pretend to be asleep. She'd relent without too much protest and he'd have his way.

It would be a disgusting few minutes to endure, but nothing she hadn't already experienced. All she had to do was think about something else, like what she'd do after she was rid of the fetus. Start a new life with her new name.

Everything went just as she'd planned it. Rodney came into her room, forced himself on her then fell asleep. She spent a half hour in the shower getting clean, smiling

Searching for Rachel

about what she'd accomplished. Men were easy to handle once you knew their motivation. And she had Rodney's number pegged.

Later, she dropped a few hints about being under age making their recent encounter a rape. If she mentioned this to her sister, she'd surely tell the police and good old Rodney would be hauled off to jail. She'd told him all this then said she was willing to keep quiet, but there was a price.

Good old boy Rodney had to find a steady job quick to make some money, or go to jail. Liz's plan worked. At first he'd complained and called her a few vulgar names. He'd said she was willing and therefore it wasn't actually rape. She'd countered with, "You'd better read up on the law, dipshit. Sex with anyone under age, consensual or not, is still classified as rape and carries a heavy jail sentence. Hell, you'd probably look good in them prison stripes they make you wear," she'd countered. She'd learned that bit about the law by visiting the local library and looking it up.

After that, she was rid of Rodney hanging around the trailer during the day. It gave her some time to be alone. And Rodney was now secretly making a few payments to keep her quiet. He was also convinced that Liz was an evil person to be feared. She in turn had nothing to fear from Rodney who kept his distance and stopped his filthy language in front of her. In fact, he'd appeared to be a changed person.

So, at the age of 15, Liz Miller learned to become a whore and a blackmailer. In time she'd also become a street prostitute. It was a hard life, not to her liking. And much later, she'd be a waitress, just like her older sister. Eventually Liz moved from Memphis to Nashville and found a job at the Huddle House there. The decision to leave Memphis and her sister was mutual. Liz's sister had become suspicious, thinking there was something going on between her and Rodney. Perhaps because Rodney was so openly keeping his distance, no longer teasing her as he once did. He acted too different from his old self. And, he wasn't staying drunk all the time now that he had a job and was helping out with the bills. Even though the new Rodney wasn't all that much better, he was all her sister had. Now that the baby was aborted, it was time to move on, get a new life; perhaps find someone whose character was better than Rodney's. Leaving her sister was Liz's last contact with any of her family. Scaring Rodney, with her threats of going to the police, was to her way of thinking a parting gift to her sister.

Using her worldly knowledge of men, and how they lusted after younger women, prompted, Liz to always dress provocatively, revealing just enough to arouse her male customers while working as a waitress. She was fully aware that women didn't appreciate the way she looked, or the way she walked, and they usually avoided her area.

She made it a point to bend over the booths to give the men a good look down the front of her uniform, knowing they were ogling her boobs. When she'd bend over, to pick up dirty dishes, she also gave them a nice view of her buns and the outline of her panties. As a result, Liz got a lot of looks as well as a lot of big tips. She enjoyed a steady group of customers who insisted on sitting in the area where she served. Barry was among that interested group.

The other waitresses couldn't compete. Behind her back they called her names and tried to ignore her, but all that failed to have any affect on Liz. Over time, she became one of the best waitresses the Huddle House ever had. She flirted openly and made three times the tips any of the other waitresses made. She didn't care what anyone thought.

Many of her customers would stop in for a cup of coffee and leave her a dollar tip. Her customers ranged from on-duty police officers to truck drivers, deliverymen, post office workers and clerks from nearby businesses. She knew most by their first names and knew what they all secretly wanted. She winked frequently and gave each of them a knowing smile.

Whenever she dated, she made it clear the sex wasn't free. It sure beat walking the streets like she'd done in Memphis for several years. She liked the fact that she didn't have to pay taxes on what she made on the side, which was actually more than she made as a waitress. The Huddle House was her spider web. She vowed she'd never work the streets again. This was much easier and safer.

One day while working at the Huddle House, she remembered a group of nicely dressed gentlemen came in and sat at one of her booths. That's how she happened to meet Barry Greene. She could feel his eyes on her backside as she walked away. She also knew he'd be asking her out soon. He never took his eyes off her she noticed.

Barry was the kind of guy she'd been looking for. He was cute, dressed well and later she learned he worked nearby, selling expensive new cars. It was several weeks before Barry asked her for a date. He took her to dinner at a nice restaurant and later, they stopped by another place where recording country and western artists hung out. Liz got several autographs and a lot of looks. She also drank more than she intended.

Barry had to help her to the car and later into her shabby apartment. She was surprised that he hadn't taken advantage of her condition and made any sexual advances that night. He was almost the perfect gentleman. She later recalled that he'd helped her into bed, helped her remove her dress and shoes, admired her bare legs and kissed her goodnight. He made up for the gentleman act on the next date, however. He arrived early holding a bottle of wine

and a pizza. For some strange reason, Liz decided not to charge Barry for the sex; she never mentioned it.
She did, however, mention that she was dating several other men. She was surprised that he didn't appear to be jealous. She liked that. Meanwhile, he was the only one getting free sex. Everyone else paid. She was saving to buy a decent automobile and instinctively knew that Barry would help her find one. In time, he mentioned that he'd taken in a nice clean car on trade and perhaps she'd like to take a look at it, after work. Anything was better than the beater she was driving. She liked it and Barry graciously made the down payment for her, just as she'd hoped he would. Eventually, he'd make a few of the payments on it as well.

None of the people who worked with Barry knew about their relationship. Barry wanted to keep it a secret, which was fine with Liz. Whenever Barry ate at the Huddle House with his friends, he always left her a five-dollar tip. She heard him get a few wise cracks from his buddies about being hot for her. "Hurry back," was her favorite parting as she quickly scooped up her tip before anyone else saw it. Sometimes when she'd leave the check, she'd linger long enough to say, "Anything else you'd like?" It was a great way to tease the guys who would often reply, "Oh yeah, there is." That's how she played her game. Sometimes the married guys would whisper and ask for her phone number. She always gave them the number at the Huddle House. Consequently, she got a lot of phone messages. Barry was among a select few who had her home number.

Searching for Rachel

Chapter 12

Barry Greene had the distinct feeling he was being followed. He hated being so paranoid. Ezra was out to ruin him, he knew, and would stop at nothing to accomplish that personal mission. In the beginning, Barry thought he'd been successful in sucking up to the old man. His brief real estate success, with a competitor of sorts, had impressed Rachel and her father. He'd done his best to charm Maureen, to get her on his side. And later, He'd anticipated being offered a job with Ezra's organization, and the plan had worked. He hadn't been able to anticipate what life would be like later. The old saying, *you don't just marry the person, you also marry into their family*, certainly turned out to be true, with one exception, Barry was never quite a member of the family.

He still missed the car business and all his friends back in Nashville. Those were fun days. Meeting Rachel had been his big ticket to better things. For a long time Barry had a distinct feeling that somehow, in some way, he'd meet someone with lots of money. It was the primary reason he sold Beamers instead of Chevy trucks. He knew from the beginning that Rachel was spoiled and made allowances for that. What annoyed him the most was his in-laws constantly hovering around, arriving unannounced, dropping in whenever they felt like it, which was often.

They were smothering his privacy. He hated that they were always suggesting what he and Rachel should be doing to raise their son. And, always bribing the kid with gifts, taking him and Rachel with them on trips, never inviting him.

Rachel didn't see what was happening to their son, but he could see it. They argued about it all the time. The only argument Barry had won was about Jake. He was furious when he learned that Maureen had bought a puppy for Jonathan, without ever checking with him beforehand. Barry never cared for dogs, or cats. Now Maureen had the dog, and the dog poop was in their yard now, not his. Even that move backfired, because Jonathan wanted to see and play with Jake all the time, just one more reason to be at his grandparents' house.

Building their dream house started out as a great fun project while they lived in an apartment. It was in a building complex Ezra owned so there was no rent. Rachel had definite ideas of what she wanted and that was okay with Barry. Rachel wanted her own studio where she could paint. It had to have skylights for the added natural light. And, all the appliances had to be stainless steel. All the cabinet and door hardware had to look like pewter, to match the sconces and light fixtures. The more he reflected on it, the more he realized that he'd had very little say in building that place. It was all Rachel, and her father of course.

Maureen was the quiet one. She stayed out of all the house discussions and decisions.. She sided with Ezra on everything and never revealed an opinion of her own. She allowed her husband to make all the decisions, which Barry thought was fine *in his house*. But when it came to Barry's castle, the old man was a guest, and more often than not, an intruder, dropping over whenever he pleased, which was too often to suit Barry. Each visit was more like an inspection. It didn't help that they lived within walking distance of each other. Rachel jogged every morning stopping by her parents' home to get Jake. Barry knew that Maureen would never walk the dog, not that he cared. Whenever Ezra arrived with Maureen, they always drove. Maureen didn't like to walk even though the walking would have been beneficial. There were a few times when Barry and Rachel were about to engage in a sexual romp when he'd hear a car door slam and knew they had company. They had to dress quickly and run downstairs to greet them. The last time that happened, Barry walked into the living room wearing a terry robe, hoping they'd get the message. By then he was beyond caring.

"You weren't in bed at this hour were you?" Ezra had asked.

"Barry was just about to jump into the shower when he heard your car," Rachel replied, looking nervously at Barry. She knew he was annoyed and probably feared what he might say to her father. He should have said, "Bad timing". Maureen would have known the meaning, even if Ezra would have ignored the remark.

Barry recalled Ezra remarking, "Well don't let us keep you from something as important as that," With that, Barry immediately left the room and went back upstairs, closing the bedroom door behind him. It was all he could do to contain his anger and not shout at his in-laws to leave.

Barry stopped counting the number of times they arrived just after dinner, as Barry was getting Rachel into a romantic mood with a second glass of wine and some of her favorite music. Jonathan would be upstairs in his room watching television, or playing. As soon as Ezra's car door would slam closed, Jonathan would come rushing down the stairs in his pajamas to greet his grandfather as he walked in the front door, even before Barry could get there.

Sometimes he'd just look up and there they were, hugging Jonathan and talking to Rachel as though Barry wasn't in the room. He'd become the invisible man, in his own home.

One day Barry learned that Ezra had acquired the mortgage on their house. Ezra had gone to the bank and bought the damn mortgage! It was the ultimate act of control and Barry hated the way he was being manipulated. Ezra explained that it was to eliminate the interest being paid, which meant a lower monthly payment. Except the payment now went to Ezra instead of the bank. Barry knew it was the price one paid for marrying into money, when you didn't have any of your own. That was the primary motivation for Barry to become successful. He had to rise above the constant pressure Ezra imposed on him.

At the office, Ezra would drop in and order him to do something unimportant in front of the staff, making him feel insignificant. It was humiliating. And later, he'd see the snickers and hear the whispering behind his back. It was a lot to endure, and over time, it wore on him. Rachel wasn't sensitive to any of it. In fact, she was oblivious to any of the problems Barry faced at work. When she had a problem, daddy always took care of it. Barry would learn about it later. Ezra would later comment something like, "I had a repair man go out and fix it knowing that you aren't particularly handy around the house." It should have pleased him, but he didn't see it that way. Barry saw it as another event where he wasn't needed.

Moving to Ocala put enough distance between Barry and the past so that he could once again breathe, make a few independent decisions. He knew people would be critical of him for moving away. Perhaps even think he was guilty in some fashion as Ezra kept suggesting. Well, there was nothing he could do about that. He had to start a new life in a new place, with new friends. In the friends

Searching for Rachel

category, Amanda McBride popped instantly to mind. There was something different about her, something slightly mysterious that intrigued him. It was time for another visit to Harry's. Perhaps he'd stay for dinner. The menu at Harry's featured several New Orleans-style dishes. Ever since Barry and Rachel visited New Orleans, on their honeymoon, Barry was hooked on blackened seafood and steaks. Barry had heard that Harry's did them just right. They also had a few Cajun specialties to test his stamina for spicy food. Maybe he'd try the grilled sausage on top of a bed of red beans and rice. He'd seen someone eating it the last time he was there and thought at the time that he'd try it on his next visit. Barry loved red beans and rice.

Thinking about New Orleans, Barry thought about his old buddy, Reggie.

Barry wasn't sure if there was a tap on his phone. He wouldn't put it past Ezra to hire someone to do that. Well, staying one step ahead of that old geezer was the name of the game now. Barry used the office phone and his cell phone for all business and personal calls. He kept abreast of the Nashville news by going to the library and reading the Nashville newspaper there. He also used the computers at the library, rather than his laptop, to check his email messages.

He always sat with his back to the counter, facing the entrance to the library. That way, he could see who came in and if anyone was taking special interest in *him*. It didn't take long to recognize most of the regular visitors to the library and that helped. A stranger would likely stand out, particularly a stranger looking for Barry. Barry would likely spot the stranger first. It was more difficult going to the post office to get his mail. Most of the people coming and going appeared to be strangers. He checked his mail at different times so he wouldn't get into a routine that could be anticipated. When he drove, he constantly checked the rearview mirror and took several different routes to the office and home. He wasn't going to make it easy for anyone keeping tabs on him.

Searching for Rachel

Chapter 13

Ezra Rueben was eager to hear another report from Nick. He'd left several messages on Nick's cell phone. On his way back to Cookeville, after Nick decided to make a swing through Smithville where in checked in with the sheriff's office. Carol said she had to work late, which gave Nick some spare time, not that he wanted to spend it talking with Ezra, but he might learn something else since Ezra wasn't prone to giving a complete picture. Rather, he gave just enough to get Nick started. That was annoying. Driving up to Ezra's house, Nick saw Ezra's Lincoln Town Car parked in the driveway. Nick felt this might be a good test in determining how the rest of the relationship would progress. He always had the option of quitting the assignment, something he didn't like to do.

"So what have you learned so far?" Ezra asked, standing in the open front door.

"Well I'm working on a theory that I'm not ready to reveal yet, mainly because I need more proof. If I'm wrong, I don't want my thoughts to impact any actions taken by you, or the police. May I come in, or do you prefer me to stand here?"

"Cut the crap. Just lay it out. I'm prepared for the worst." Ezra backed up and motioned for Nick to come inside. "You agree now that Barry had something to do with my daughter's disappearance don't you?"

"I think that's a distinct possibility. And, it may have been planned in advance. And, there may even be an accomplice. I'll know better after I've been down to New Orleans and then to Ocala to check out Barry."

"What good do you honestly think that will do? I told you already that I have someone keeping a constant surveillance on Barry's movements. I can show you those reports to save some time, not to mention the added expense."

"Mr. Rueben, I have my own method of conducting an investigation. I don't want to keep repeating that. If you care to check, my track record has been pretty good over the years. I achieved that record by being thorough, checking small details that everyone else overlooked."

"Okay, what have you discovered that others missed so far?"

Nick had to think how he wanted to answer that question. He had two missing women, a missing trunk and a missing vehicle, plus a few unresolved questions. To keep Ezra satisfied, Nick went with the trunk. Perhaps Maureen had already mentioned it. If not, he'd use that as his example of overlooked items. He was sure there would be more.

"Do you recall a trunk being in the upstairs guest bedroom of the house?" Nick asked.

"Of course. Maureen and Rachel were out shopping one day last year and found it in an antique shop. Maureen bought it to store some of Jonathan's toys. Why?"

"Well it's no longer in the house. There's an indentation in the carpeting where it used to be. I think Rachel moved it later to the houseboat. Were you aware of that?"

"No. I haven't been on the houseboat for a while. Is it there now?"

"No, I didn't find it anywhere and I looked closely."
"Then how did you know it was a trunk that was missing?"
"Because, I found a tray that inserts into a trunk. I've seen many similar trays and recognized it. I also found blankets in a closet, stacked on the floor. I suspect those blankets were being stored in the trunk."
"Hmmm. That's certainly strange. I'll ask Maureen if she knows anything about that trunk being moved to the houseboat. What else did you learn?"
"I think Barry kept in touch with some of his friends at the car dealership in Nashville. There's a lead that needs to be followed up over there."
"I'm aware that he took Wednesday afternoons off to play golf with some of his pals in Nashville. It always annoyed me that he put such a high priority on his golf game over business. You don't sell real estate on the golf course. Stock brokers and insurance salesmen might make sales that way, but not real estate people."
"I need to look into those Wednesday golf games."
Nick was a little surprised that Ezra, being the suspicious person he was, hadn't checked out Barry's excuse for being gone on Wednesdays.
"And what would you expect to learn, his golf handicap?"
"Mr. Rueben, I think I've already explained my position and how I work. I'll keep you posted on anything important."
"No, you'll keep me posted on every little piece of information you pick up that has any bearing on Barry being guilty. Once we can prove it, I'll see that he gets his just dessert… in hell."
"Let me give you some good advice. Be very careful what you say and do with regards to your son-in-law. If it

turns out that he's innocent, and that's still a possibility, he'll have one hell of a lawsuit against you for slander."

"But he's not innocent! He's guilty. And that's what I'm paying you for, to find out how we can prove it beyond a shadow of a doubt."

"Excuse me, I must have missed something. I thought I was looking for your missing daughter. As for your son-in-law, I think you've already made up your mind, regardless of any evidence. We have to be careful, very careful not to break the law, or intrude on his rights. Your lawyer would tell you the same thing."

"The hell he would. My lawyer does exactly what I tell him to do. If the rules need bending, he knows how to do it, believe me. I pay him enough."

"Okay. Is there anything else I need to know that you haven't mentioned?"

"Like what?"

"Like the name and address of the detective agency you have in Ocala. You might call them and tell them I'll be checking in with them sometime soon."

"So you think you'll find something they haven't uncovered?"

"I'll know that once I've been there. I rarely speculate." *That wasn't true.*

"Really?"

"Not to the extent that it will cause a problem."

"But you have a hunch about something, don't you?"

"Maybe. I'll get into that with you later. By the way, did Barry or Rachel mention they were planning on spending the weekend on your houseboat?"

"I don't remember if they did, or not now. Barry had a set of keys and used it more than I did. Rachel may have said something to Maureen, I don't know."

"By the way, since the search seems to have ended in New Orleans, did you hire anyone down there to do some checking around?" Nick could almost guess the answer.

"Yes, his name is Herschel Fielding. He came highly recommended, but he didn't turn up anything. I'll give you his address as well."

Nick was exhausted by the time he left Ezra Rueben's house. Maureen Rueben never came into the study, but she was in the entryway to say goodbye when he left. If she had anything to add, Nick was unable to tell. Ezra was the spokes-person for the family. He had to be one domineering son of a bitch. Nick wasn't sure he'd be able to put up with a father-in-law like that. He was beginning to understand why Barry left Smithville.

Carol Mayberry listened intently as Nick gave her a summary of his day and bounced his theory on her. He knew that she'd never reveal any part of the conversation to anyone. He trusted her completely. She was one of only a few people he did trust, and it helped him put his thoughts in order.

"Nick, do you think the husband killed his wife, put her in that trunk and dropped it into the lake somewhere?" Carol asked.

"That's a possibility. The trunk is missing, Rachel is missing and so is his girlfriend from the Huddle House. There's a connection somewhere."

"Did you mention the girlfriend to Mr. Rueben?"

"No. I deliberately left that out. He's so darned impatient, he'd have someone searching for her tomorrow."

"Well what's so bad about that?"

"I don't want him second guessing me, or getting in my way. For all we know, Rachel may have met someone in New Orleans, or she could have been involved in an accident and nobody has made the connection yet." *Or she may have gone to have an abortion, but why go all that far away?* Nick didn't voice those thoughts.

"Speaking as a woman, I'd say she's dead. Otherwise, she would have been in touch with her parents and her son. No mother leaves her child suddenly like that, even if she had a boyfriend, or was secretly seeing someone else."

"I agree with you. It bothers me that she never called her parents, yet she supposedly called Barry. We have no real proof it was Rachel who called. It could have been his girlfriend Liz who made the call, knowing the police would check the phone records. It certainly helped him establish an alibi and diverted police attention to another area, away from here." If that's what Barry planned, then Nick was dealing with a shrewd, and perhaps ruthless, individual. And the closer he got to the truth, the more dangerous the situation.

Nick wondered why Rachel hadn't used her cell phone to call Barry. Calling collect from a traceable pay phone only helped to reinforce Barry's alibi. *If she was there, and he was here, he couldn't have had anything to do with her disappearance... unless, he hired someone.* It was this alibi that was saving Barry at the moment.

"When you talk with Barry, you should ask him, why he never tried to find his wife in New Orleans, after she called. I would have thought he'd ask where she was staying. It's a logical question for a husband, or a wife to ask," Carol said.

"Yes. Thank you for bringing up that very important point." Talking to Carol always helped Nick to organize his thoughts. "Any chance you can get free for a few days… to take a trip with me down to the Big Easy?"

"I was wondering when you'd ask." Carol gave him a knowing smile. They knew each other well enough to anticipate each other's thoughts and comments. She could finish Nick's sentences and follow his line of reasoning. It was such a comfortable feeling. It pleased her that Nick confided in her the way he did. They had no secrets and neither gave the other any cause to be jealous. It was an unspoken agreement.

Carol still thanked her lucky stars that she found the courage to flirt with Nick that day two years ago. It was something she'd never done before. They were standing in the office lobby saying goodbye. Instead of shaking his hand, Carol stepped forward to give him a hug. She remembered she also gave him a quick kiss goodbye and an impulsive whisper to "hurry back".

She'd been nervous and felt flushed afterward. It was completely out of character for her to do something like that. Months later, when she and Nick were having dinner, Nick recalled that moment and said he'd felt an instant magnetism and thought about her all the way to Atlanta. As a single guy, Nick had dated a lot of women and had an opportunity to date many more.

Yet that particular moment with Carol was unlike any other, one gentle kiss among thousands. It was the one he'd always remember. All the others were forgotten, or just a blur now. Past flings and romances were blurred memories, best to be forgotten.

Nick also wondered what might have happened had Carol not made that first bold move. Would he have called her? Probably, he thought. That final day she'd arrived at work looking particularly nice, as if she were going out later, after work. He didn't know it then that she'd dressed with particular care that day, just for him. At the time, she wasn't even aware of the fact that she was doing it for him. She was just wondering if she'd ever see him again and hoped she would. She liked Nick a lot and found him charming and handsome. Also, he hadn't tried to flirt with her or any of the other girls in the office. She liked that about him. His demeanor had been professional except for that final departing embrace. They'd both felt the subtle tingling shock of awareness. That final day was the beginning of their romantic journey that was still in progress. Carol still felt excited every time Nick walked into the room. Just holding hands was a pleasurable experience. Hugging him and kissing him goodnight was a moment she always looked forward to. She loved falling asleep in his arms. She felt so safe, a feeling she'd never truly experienced before. She never wanted it to end.

Carol knew Nick was getting serious about moving to Tennessee and that suggested he was also thinking about marriage. She hoped so. The answer was *yes*, whenever he decided to ask. Meanwhile, she'd wait, letting the suspense mount and continue to enjoy each other's moods, emotions, dreams and experiences.

No other man ever made her feel so complete; so satisfied. Life without Nick was something she couldn't contemplate. He filled an empty spot in her life that she didn't even realize existed until he entered. The thought of Nick not being in her life made her feel sick to her stomach. She could feel a knot begin to materialize and had to shake the thought from her mind.

She also knew, without ever asking, that Nick wasn't seeing anyone else, even though he'd had several opportunities. Carol liked being able to have that kind of trust and secretly vowed never to do anything to make Nick jealous. She knew some women felt the need to test a relationship by flirting with other men, but she didn't. Several times she told Nick that she loved him with all her heart and he'd confessed feeling the same way.

In her mind, they were already engaged. The idea of a trip to New Orleans made her feel giddy.

Searching for Rachel

Chapter 14

Herschel Fielding's office was on the first floor of a converted three-story Victorian house in the Garden District. There were apartments on the second and third floors with a separate entrance. Nick estimated the man's weight at close to 300 pounds. The man was bald except for a small fringe of white hair over his ears. He reminded Nick of the actor, Sydney Greenestreet, who appeared in some of the old classic black and white films with Bogart playing the role of Sam Spade. The Maltese Falcon was one of Nick's favorite flicks from that era. He also reminded Nick of the late ballad singer, Burl Ives except that Herschel didn't sport a goatee. His eyes were dark and his stare was intense, as though looking into your brain. Nick thought the man probably had great concentration and recall.

"Mr. Rueben sent me a picture of his daughter. Quite a striking young woman, I must say. As you may know, Mr. Alexander, New Orleans is one of those places where people come, when they don't want to be found, or found out." The big man was leaning back in a wood desk chair that barely supported him. It creaked every time he moved.

"I've heard that. Do you have a list of the places you checked?" Nick was fascinated by the man's intense gaze. At times he detected a twinkle, then his heavy eyelids would narrow when he wanted to make a point. This wasn't a man who could be easily fooled. He was like a cobra, patiently watching before striking his victim.

"Of course. Are you suggesting I was somehow remiss in my investigation?"

"No, on the contrary. I just want to eliminate those places, so I don't duplicate your efforts." *It was a fast save.* Nick was trying to be as polite as possible with the old gentleman. Nick had done a quick background check prior to making the trip and learned that Herschel had been a prosecuting attorney at one time. He was a bachelor with a taste for expensive wines and cigars. He walked with a cane, but some suspected it was mostly for protection should he need to wield it. Never the less, a cane could come in handy, even for walking, when one weighed 300 pounds or more.

The man probably knew every crack and cranny of the city where a person could hide. Having been in the business a long time, he had to have numerous contacts. In no way did Nick want to give the impression he was there to cause any trouble for Mr. Fielding, or question his ability. Staying on the friendly side of the big man was just good common sense.

"You have quite a unique knack of putting things… for a Yankee, Mr. Alexander. I think you've spent considerable time in the south."

"Thank you. I'm trying to make the adjustment. My girlfriend is a strong influence. She lives in Tennessee."

"Southern belles can do that. Yes, they certainly can. I congratulate you on your good taste. By any chance, did you bring her along on this trip?"

"Yes I did. She's doing a little shopping at the moment. I think she would have been delighted to meet you. I'm sorry I didn't bring her with me today."

Searching for Rachel

"Well we can remedy that oversight. Allow me to invite you both to dine with me tonight. I know all the best places to eat." *I'm sure you do*, Nick thought.

"That would be great. I appreciate the offer and accept." Nick knew he had to go slow with this shrewd gentleman who put grace before business. To rush things would be a mistake. Besides, having a personal guide to some of the better eating establishments wasn't a bad idea. Carol would be ~~impressed~~ LIKE THAT.

Dinner was a two-hour affair in a quaint restaurant in the French Quarter. All the waiters wore tuxedos. They were seated in a lower level, walking down one flight of steps from the street. From the outside, the restaurant was unremarkable in the middle of the block and easy to overlook. Two gas lamps and a Greene canvas awning over the entrance suggested an elegant surprise hidden within. The food was superb and the wine Herschel ordered was from his own private stock kept there.

Nick noticed that Carol hadn't stopped smiling since they arrived. She was definitely ~~impressed~~ and enjoying every minute. A waiter remained near their table during the entire meal refilling their water glasses and making sure everything was satisfactory. Nick wasn't used to such VIP treatment. His steak was one of the best he'd ever had. He couldn't quite identify the spices and herbs used and refused to ask. Instead he took his time and enjoyed every morsel. He planned to leave a very big tip.

By the time the Brandy arrived, Herschel was ready to discuss business. He offered Nick a cigar. When Nick reluctantly refused, mainly because he didn't want to offend Carol, who didn't like smoking, Herschel put the cigar in his breast pocket to enjoy later. He just nodded that he understood. Nick knew that the subject of Rachel would surface eventually and was patient. Without having to ask, Herschel gave Nick a two-page list of places he'd

TIP IS FIK THE SERWICE

checked. He also listed the names of his contacts. It was an *impressive* report."

"If you ask me, Mr. Rueben got his money's worth. I'm not here to check up on you Herschel. However, I'd like to enlist your help with a similar assignment."

"Ah, the intrigue continues." The great man rubbed his hands together in anticipation. "You have some additional information to impart?"

"Yes, and I trust this will remain just between the two of us for the present. I will pay you for your help in assisting me to find yet another woman. Her name is Liz Miller. She may go by Elizabeth, or even Lisa. She looks a lot like the missing Rachel. She could have blond hair, or it could be dyed red. She was formerly a waitress in Nashville and may be working in a similar capacity here. Turns out she left her last job quite suddenly."

"And you think she might be here in New Orleans?"

"It's a possibility I need to explore."

"Is it possible she's hiding from someone?"

"Yes that's also possible."

"And is this woman's disappearance in any way connected to the other woman we've been looking for?"

"That too is possible. I think there may be a connection. At least they're both connected to Barry Greene. He was married to one, and seeing the other on the side. Both suddenly disappeared about the same time."

"That's quite an interesting coincidence. Any chance Mr. Rueben learned about this tart waitress and paid her off to get lost?"

That thought had never occurred to Nick. It totally surprised him.

"Yes, knowing Ezra's disposition, it's quite possible. He's a very suspicious man and could easily have had someone following Barry in Nashville. Barry supposedly played golf on Wednesdays with some of his friends. I think it may have been just an excuse to see his girlfriend. I don't know that for a fact, I'm just guessing."

"I'm wondering why this woman you call Liz, would select New Orleans to hide. Surely there are places much closer. Birmingham for example is just a few hours away and so is Memphis."

"If Barry killed his wife, he needs an alibi for the time she disappeared. Liz may have provided the alibi by posing as Rachel. If so, then she flew here and called him later... collect. That helped to divert the search from where Rachel may have actually disappeared. Barry may have killed her and disposed of the body earlier. He needed an established alibi to eliminate being the prime suspect. He wanted the investigation to shift to someplace away from Smithville and the Center Hill Lake."

"It's an interesting theory. It also makes this Liz an accomplice to a possible murder, which it is beginning to smell like. What would keep this Liz from blackmailing Barry later?"

"Nothing. Barry can't afford to have her talking to Ezra, or the police. If she's still alive, she may very well be hiding from Barry, knowing that she's a potential threat."

"This is indeed an intriguing case you're on, Nick." They were on a first name basis now. "Do I send my bill to you, or to Mr. Rueben?"

"Send it to me. I'm the one who's hiring you for this assignment. If it proves to be a dead end, I'll absorb the expense."

"Don't be foolish my dear man. Mr. Rueben wouldn't expect you to do that. He may be a bastard in many ways, but he's a businessman and understands necessary expenses. He paid me very well for what I did. I won't charge you the same rate I charged him. Who knows, I may need to use your services one day and you can return the favor." He followed this with a deep chuckle.

Nick saw the twinkle in the man's eyes that disguised how truly shrewd he was, perhaps even dangerous, depending on one's relationship.

"I certainly will look forward to returning the favor," Nick said. He had a feeling that Herschel dealt heavily in favors. Probably half the top tier of city officials owed him a favor or two, Nick thought.

"Nick, I have one more question to pose. I hope this doesn't offend you, Carol. Forgive me for my suspicious ways, but is it possible, that at one time Ezra had an incestuous relationship with his daughter? Because, if he did, it might explain why she left. She might actually be running from her father, rather than her husband."

"It's funny that you would ask that. It crossed my mind when I learned how spoiled she was. She may have teased him to get what she wanted when she was younger. And maybe Barry found out about it. That would certainly be cause for a good spat. But I would think Barry would take advantage of that situation and confront the old man. It would insure his future." *Or end it quickly, not unlike what was happening.*

"Yes, that makes sense. I'm sorry I brought it up. It was just a flicker on my aging yet suspicious brain."

"Please don't apologize. It's that kind of thinking that adds new perspective. Sometimes we get so focused we forget to look at other possibilities," Nick said.

"Nick, you would have made a first class prosecutor."

"Thank you, but I always preferred to be on the seek and catch end of things."

Searching for Rachel

Chapter 15

Nick Alexander no longer had any doubts about Herschel Fielding's investigative abilities. It was apparent the man knew everyone of any importance, and a few seedy types as well. It was his stock in trade. Nick learned a bit more about Herschel's reputation from a captain on the New Orleans police force when he stopped by earlier.

Herschel had a taxi waiting and the driver seemed to know him. In fact, Herschel seemed to know the driver's name as well, calling him Dooley. Nick and Carol declined the offer to ride. Instead, they opted to walk back to their hotel taking in the exotic sights, listening to all the music blaring and people laughing from behind open windows and darkened doorways. It was an atmosphere shrouded in mystery and excitement. Nick walked close to Carol with his arm around her waist. At one point he slowly lowered his hand to massage her buns. She didn't pull away or resist his amorous gesture. Any place else it would have seemed entirely inappropriate, here it didn't.

"Want to fool around?" Nick whispered.

"I thought that's what you were doing," Carol giggled.

"That's just a preview of sexier things to come."

"Then maybe we'd better hurry, before you lose interest."

"Not a chance!" They'd had a romantic encounter earlier, before getting dressed for dinner, and now he was looking forward to a repeat performance. They were staying in a quaint two-story hotel in the French Quarter. It was the only hotel Nick had ever stayed in that put satin sheets on the beds. There were scented candles in the bathroom and expensive smelling soap. The towels were big and fluffy. These were the extra items that only an expensive hotel would offer in contrast to most of the ordinary places he stayed. For this particular trip, Nick felt that the added expense was well worth the special effect it created. Had Carol not been with him, he would have stayed at a more modest place.

He planned to sleep late, then, treat Carol to a delicious brunch at another famous restaurant, The Court of Two Sisters. Before leaving, they'd spend a few hours at the casino a few blocks away. Maybe he'd get lucky. As it stood, Nick felt he'd already gotten luckier than he deserved, thanks to Carol's feminine intuition and sensuous touch. New Orleans would always remain a romantic fantasy in Nick's memory.

Carol was having similar thoughts. For the first time in her life she approached Nick with shameless abandon wearing a black see-through lacy garment she'd found while he was meeting with Herschel earlier. It remained on her body for a total of 45 seconds, the time it took Nick to get completely naked. Their coupling became a series of sexual adventures that lasted throughout the night interrupted with short periods of sleep.

The following morning they both suffered mild hangovers and sore muscles. It was the price they paid for overindulgence the night before. They'd overindulged in food, drink and sex. Consequently, Nick couldn't complain about how he felt. He was about to ask Carol if she wanted an encore, even though it would be just teasing, then decided not to ask, for fear she might actually accept the challenge. He'd need at least a day to recuperate before becoming partially recharged. Olympic sex wasn't something he was up to on an every week basis.

Instead of joining Carol in the shower, he remained in bed listening to the water run and hearing Carol humming a familiar song. He'd never heard Carol sing or hum in the shower before. He had heard her make other sounds when he was with her, washing her backside while she shampooed her hair. Sometimes they remained in the shower until the hot water ran out. Nick loved the way Carol washed his body, treating it with loving care, gently massaging his tight muscles. She loved to tease him and acted like a surprised young girl when he responded. "Oh my, what's happening here?" she'd coyly ask. "Is this for me?"

Their stay in the French Quarter was like a perfect honeymoon. Nick decided it was time to ask the question that was haunting them.

"When do you want to get married?" he asked, when Carol returned from the shower with just an oversized towel wrapped around her. She had another towel wrapped around her wet hair.

"You're just suggesting that as a way to get me to crawl back into bed," she said, dropping the towels and covering him with kisses. "I'm not sure this old body can take much more right now. Could I have a rain check?"

"Hey, my bed is always your bed, honey. Nobody else I want to sleep with but you."

"Yes, I guess it's time you settled down. There's no real hurry, Nick. Let's make it a long engagement and get married whenever it strikes us as the right time."

Instead of going to the casino, they walked through the French Quarter exploring all the jewelry shops that were open. One particular shop specialized in antique rings, pins and pendants. Carol found a ring with a ruby she loved and that became her engagement ring. It fit her finger perfectly, another sign that things were meant to happen just the way events were currently unfolding. Carol kept admiring her new ring on the flight back to Nashville.

"I feel as though we were just on our honeymoon," she whispered, holding Nick's hand. He was pretending to sleep, hoping it would be a shorter flight that way.

"Does that mean I get to sleep all night tonight?"

"Spoken like an old married man, but the answer is no. I have great expectations and know you'll fulfill your end of the bargain nicely."

"Oh Lord, I think I'm in trouble," Nick groaned. "I'd better eat a ton of oysters for dinner."

"Sorry. The best place for eating oysters was back in New Orleans, not in Cookeville. You'd better just take a nap and have a sweet dream. We'll pick up some fresh shrimp at the supermarket when we get home."

"Good, because I absolutely hate oysters." With that, Nick fell asleep still holding her hand. Carol provided a good distraction since Nick hated to fly. Being somewhat exhausted from the night before, he fell into a deep sleep until they arrived back in Nashville.

Nick left Carol to wait for their luggage while he made a fast trip to the airport police office. He wanted to inquire about Liz's missing Honda Civic. They could quickly check to see if it had been left in any of the parking areas. And they would also be able to get the registration information as well. Nothing turned up.

Searching for Rachel

Chapter 16

Barry Greene was convinced now, after the private investigator's visit, that he was being watched. Consequently he made sure his daily routine didn't change. He dropped off Jonathan at his school, stopped by a nearby deli for coffee and a bagel and was in the office by 9:00, unless the traffic was particularly heavy. Rush hour in Ocala could cause delays, particularly on the major routes crisscrossing the town. Visitor traffic clustered near the I-75 exits where the motels and fast food restaurants could be found.

He made a habit of eating lunch at different places then spending an hour or so driving through various neighborhoods. This gave him a better sense of where the modest, medium and higher priced houses were located. The horse farms were on the far outskirts. Barry also made it a point to play a few rounds of golf at all the available courses so he could comment on them with some personal knowledge when asked by prospects.

Another trick he used was to post a few of his business cards on public bulletin boards in all the grocery stores and shopping centers. Barry made a point of visiting all the desk clerks at the better motels and told them to give out his card to anyone thinking about moving into the area. The clerk was to write their name on the back of the card and Barry promised to give them a gift certificate to the Cracker Barrel for each card he received back. As a newcomer to the area himself, he had to use any and all means to become established. He'd done the same thing when he sold cars.

Barry sometimes felt like he was leading two separate lives. During working hours he had to be friendly and outgoing, all the while being suspicious of strangers who weren't prospects. He confined his private time to a few special locations where in time he recognized the local patrons. But, the paranoia remained, even increased. It bothered him that the private investigator had found out about Liz. Even though Liz was out of the picture now, his association with her suggested a possible motive for Rachel's disappearance, and Ezra would surely use that against him. It also bothered him that this new investigator seemed to have a lot of confidence. He asked questions to which Barry felt he already knew the answers. That meant he was judging Barry's reaction. The Liz announcement had caught him off-guard and he was sure his surprise registered. He didn't like appearing guilty to anyone.

Liz's disappearance had cost him $5,000. And he did indeed owe Reggie a big one for his help.

Most of all, he worried about Jonathan. If Ezra wanted to, he could hire someone to snatch the boy as he was leaving school. Better yet, the old man could do it himself with success. All he had to do was bring along Jake. Jonathan would be gone in a heartbeat. In many ways Barry wondered why Ezra hadn't made the attempt by now. The fact that it hadn't happened wasn't sufficient reason to let his guard down. He had to be wary at all times.

And that put a real kink in his social life.

Barry had been fortunate to find a widow, Mrs. Pearlman who was willing to baby sit for Jonathan whenever Barry had to work late. She agreed to drive to

Searching for Rachel

school and meet him on those occasions. Barry always instructed Jonathan in advance to look for Mrs. Pearlman who would then take the boy back to her house. Having a dog, a mixed breed named Sparky, was another nice plus. Since Jonathan didn't have Jake around to play with, Sparky served as a good substitute.

Within a few weeks' time Mrs. Pearlman was watching Jonathan on a daily basis after school and frequently giving him his dinner as well. Barry said that his early evenings were becoming the best time to show houses, which was a lie. He just needed to socialize a little. Barry started checking out all the bars in search of some easy action. He had the names, and phone numbers, of a few local ladies who would have been easy enough to spend an night with, but they just didn't appeal to him for anything more than a one night stand, so he passed rather than get involved with them. Happy hour at Harry's on the square was becoming his favorite place to relax. The bar side filled up by five and those staying for dinner were taken to the dining room other side of the bar, or they could eat outside if it wasn't too cool.

It didn't take long before Barry recognized most of the regular patrons. He also noticed a lot of good-looking businesswomen hanging out there. He was hoping to run into Amanda again. The casual atmosphere suited him. Soon he was nodding to people who also recognized him as a regular. Barry made it a point to sit near the end of the bar so he could face the entrance and still watch CNN on the monitor overhead.

While hoping to see Amanda, Barry noticed a tall, middle-aged man reading a magazine while he ate dinner. He was sitting alone at a raised table in the bar section. Barry caught him looking over at him a few times. Later, Barry spotted the same man seated at the library reading a newspaper. He was a stranger and Barry instantly knew he was being watched. When Barry left the library, after using the computer, the man got up and immediately approached the librarian behind the counter.

"The man who just left was using that computer over there." Nick pointed to the unit. "I need to use that same machine for a little while." Nick gave the woman one of his business cards and she registered some surprise.

"Has he done something wrong?"

"Don't know that yet. I'll know soon enough."

"Can you tell me why he's being investigated?"

"Perhaps later, not right now. I'd prefer it if you didn't mention this to anyone right now."

"Is he one of those, you know, sexual predators or something like that?"

"Not to my knowledge. It's a different type of investigation."

Nick sat at the computer, reached into his jacket pocket and removed a disc. It was a special disc with a program that allowed him to track all the recent activity, even deleted items. A hacker had sold it to him. It took awhile to sort through all the unimportant items. There was an email message from Keith, it was a follow up to an earlier alert to Barry about a private detective who'd been in recently asking questions. Keith wanted to know if Barry was getting it on with Liz. *So they did keep in touch. Surprise, surprise.* And Keith knew, or suspected that Barry had a relationship with Liz. Keith had lied to him without blinking. It reinforced Nick's distrust in car salesmen. He wondered if it was part of their sales training, keeping in mind that Barry was once a car salesman as well.

There was another brief email message from someone who called himself Reggie reminding Barry that he "owed him a big one". *Owed for what?*

Searching for Rachel

Nick inserted another disc that allowed him to track the email sender a New Orleans service provider. Reggie was someone in New Orleans whom Barry owed a big favor. *So the possibility of an accomplice was emerging.* Nick sent an email message with this information to Herschel, so he could check it out at his end.

Next, Nick dropped by Barry's condo. He already knew where Barry lived having checked it out earlier. Nick saw Barry's Ford Explorer parked outside in front of the entrance. Barry opened the front door and was surprised to see the same man who'd been in the restaurant and the library earlier. Obviously the man had been following him.

"What do you want?" Barry asked.

"It's time we had a little talk, Barry. May I come in?" Nick didn't wait for an answer, just pushed past Barry and walked into the living room. Nick sized up the room and sat on the cream-colored leather couch as though he'd been invited. Nick crossed his legs and motioned Barry to sit. Barry remained standing with his arms folded across his chest.

"Did Ezra send you down here to spy on me?"

"I don't spy on people. I merely observe them, something akin to a portrait photographer. People reveal interesting insights into themselves by the way they walk and talk. Being an old car salesman, you already know all that. You know how to walk the walk and talk the talk, don't you, Barry?" *And I'll bet you can tell a good lie without blinking, looking me straight in the eye, just like your buddy Keith.*

"If you say so. And you find me particularly interesting, is that it?"

"Yes, you're an interesting guy, Barry. Your wife disappears and you don't seem to be the least bit upset about it. I find that just a little strange actually."

"Well I am upset about it. Damned upset. I'm also upset that you're here harassing me. I have a father-in-law from hell to contend with...."

"Yes, I've met him, and I guess I don't envy you that relationship. I've been hired to help find out what happened to Rachel. You should know that I'm very good at what I do. And I assure you that when I'm finished, we'll have all the answers. It's just a matter of time."

"Well good luck. And, you're not very good. I spotted you at Harry's watching me. I also saw you watching me at the library."

"Getting a little paranoid there, Barry? I know you saw me watching you. I wasn't trying to hide it from you. I wanted you to know that you were being watched."

"Well as you can see, I don't have anything to hide. I'm just working so I can raise my kid and stay far away from Ezra's influence. So watching me is a total waste of time. I lead a boring life right now. Rachel didn't do me any favors leaving like that. And the police know everything there is to know, except where she is."

"Oh, I think they'll figure it out in time. When you were still living in Smithville, the police just didn't ask you the right questions."

"So you have it all figured out? Why don't you tell me where my wife is? I'd like to know. My son asks about her every day."

"When your wife called you from New Orleans, did you happen to ask her where she was staying?"

"Yeah, I did. She wouldn't tell me."

"Interesting. And later, you didn't make any effort to try and find her?"

"That's not true. I flew down to New Orleans and hired someone to look for her. I guess Ezra forgot to mention that. He only wants you to see the situation from his warped perspective."

"Did he know you hired someone?"

"I'd be very surprised if he didn't. He's been watching every move I make ever since Rachel and I got married."

"Oh I think he may have been watching you a little before then," Nick said. "Do the police know that you flew down to New Orleans and attempted to search for your wife?"

"I don't know, maybe. Anyway, they're not interested in me. They know I didn't have anything to do with Rachel's disappearance. She's the one who left and there is a witness who can attest to that. He saw her leave the marina." Barry remained standing. It was obvious he wanted this discussion to end quickly.

Nick didn't miss the implication. Barry was relying on the man at the marina to support his alibi. Without that, things might be very different. Nick suspected that little departure scene may have been staged.

"So what was the big argument about? The one that caused her to leave you stranded on the houseboat that Sunday?"

"Look, married people have arguments all the time, and we had our fair share of them. Mainly we argued about Ezra and Maureen. They were interfering in our life and our marriage! They were stealing my son's affection, spoiling him. The kid was spending way too much time with his grandparents. That's what we were arguing about."

"So she left and then called you two days later." It seemed like a weak explanation to Nick. "When did you go to New Orleans?"

"A couple days after that, when Ezra was telling reporters that I was responsible for his daughter's disappearance. He sure was quick to put me in a bad light, but the police didn't seem to go along with it. Otherwise why didn't they arrest me, right?"

"I don't know what the police thought. Obviously they didn't have enough to hold you as a suspect. But then they didn't know about your relationship with Liz Miller, did they?" Nick saw the surprised look on Barry's face. The man's mouth opened and his eyes opened larger. For several seconds there was silence. *Gotcha,* Nick thought.

"Hey, she's just someone who worked at a place where I used to eat, that's all."

Nick picked up on Barry using the past tense, meaning he knew Liz no longer worked at the Huddle House. His recovery was pretty good, but not convincing. He needed to take a lesson from his buddy, Keith. *You've been away from the car business too long.*

"Not according to her apartment superintendent. He said he saw you there with her on several occasions. I also find it interesting that Liz looks so much like Rachel. Dye her hair red and they'd pass for twin sisters." Nick gave Barry a knowing smirk.

"Now that you mention it, they did look a lot alike. I never put that together until now. So how is Liz?" Barry had recovered from his initial shock. Only a good car salesman, with lots of experience lying, could react that fast.

"Don't know. She's missing, too. Quit work and left town suddenly, about the same time Rachel disappeared."

"Is that right?"

"Yep. Do you suppose Ezra found out about the two of you seeing each other and sent her packing?"

"That wouldn't surprise me. But if he knew about Liz, why didn't he ever throw that in my face?"

"Probably just saving it, for the right time. He's not a man I'd want to have an ongoing fight with. Sooner, or later, you'd lose. Maybe lose everything."

Searching for Rachel

"Yeah, well we've been battling for quite some time. Which is why, I had to move here, away from all his influence. So where do you suppose Liz took off to?"

"I don't have a clue. I was hoping you'd be able to help me out there."

"Me, help you? You gotta be kidding. Like I said, I can't help you out with anything. And why would I want to? You're working for Ezra and he hates my guts. So, I guess our little chat here is over. Tell Ezra my lawyer is keeping real busy filing motions. The more he tries to harass me, the more it's going to cost him later."

Nick got up, ready to leave and said, "What's the name of the guy you hired in New Orleans?"

"His name is Harold Davis. He's a private investigator. He didn't find anything."

It was obvious to Nick that the man was scared. He was almost hyperventilating by the time Nick left. Nick gave away just enough to rattle him. He deliberately didn't mention anything about the trunk, or Rachel being pregnant. He'd save those surprises for later. Now he had one more item for Herschel to check on. When did Barry arrive and whom did he hire in New Orleans? Maybe it was this character Reggie, whom Barry owed. Owed for what, looking for Rachel, or making Liz disappear? Nick would leave those questions for Herschel.

Nick still wanted to check in with the investigator Ezra had hired in Ocala. If Liz was in Ocala, Barry was no doubt seeing her and they'd have a surveillance report. Meanwhile they could compare notes on the joys of working for Ezra Rueben.

Chapter 17

Amanda McBride was sitting in her father's office when Nick Alexander arrived. She was about to leave when she heard Nick mention Barry Greene's name.

"Dad, is Barry Greene one of our clients?" she asked.

"No, he's under surveillance for one of our clients, Ezra Rueben. I don't think you know anything about it," Charles McBride answered. "Gordon is assigned to keep an eye on him."

"That's interesting, because I recently met a Barry Greene while having a drink with one of my friends. This Barry Greene sells real estate, looks a lot like that fitness guru, Richard Simmons with the frizzy hair."

"We're talking about the same man then. What did he tell you?"

"Not much. We just met briefly over a drink. He was by himself, but I had the feeling he was looking to hook up with someone. He was kinda cool. Dressed nice. So why are we watching him?"

"Our client thinks he may have killed his wife. The wife is missing and her father is our client. Big pain in the ass, too. Calls me all the time for updates."

Nick listened to the exchange and interrupted when he started to laugh. "I'm glad to hear that I'm not the only one with that opinion. Has Barry been seen with any women?"

Nick didn't want to mention Liz for fear it would get reported back to Ezra.

"Not yet, but he's been scoping out a lot of local watering holes, so he's no doubt on the make. Our man reports that he's been acting a little nervous lately. He may have made Gordon tailing him. Gordon doesn't have to stay right behind him, we have a transponder planted on Barry's Explorer, so we always know where he is," Charles said.

"You have his phone tapped too?" Nick asked, even though he knew the answer.

"Let's just say that we've got all the bases covered here."

"That might explain why Barry is using the computers at the library to check his email messages. I think he's paranoid and knows he's being watched," Nick said.

"Well, so far, he hasn't said, or done anything that would cause an alarm."

Nick turned to Amanda and asked, "Did you give Barry one of your business cards?"

"Yeah, but not the one with this name on it. I always use my travel consultant card with strangers. I don't want people to know that I also work for my dad."

"She's good with the cheating husbands. They never suspect she's a first class pee eye," Charles said with pride.

"I would have guessed as much," Nick replied. She was young, attractive and single. Any red-blooded younger man, maybe even a middle-aged man, would go for her. There was a time when one middle-aged man in particular would have made a move in her direction, Nick thought smiling. Barry was no doubt fantasizing about her.

"If you should run into Barry again, please don't let on that you know anything about him. Who knows, he may even tell you something we can use," Nick said.

"Too bad he's suspected of something. I thought he was kinda cute. A lot of the good looking guys I meet these days turn out to be gay. That's a real bummer."

Nick had no doubts she'd find someone capable of responding to her charms. There was a time, before he'd met Carol, when he might have responded to that lament. He couldn't imagine her having any trouble finding a nice guy to spend time with.

Nick was satisfied that Barry was being baby sat at this end and that Liz wasn't anywhere nearby. If she was, Barry wouldn't be sniffing around all the local pickup spots.

Searching for Rachel

Chapter 18

Herschel Fielding was pleased to make Nick's acquaintance, and pleased with the way he'd responded, giving Herschel another assignment. He preferred working for Nick as opposed to Ezra, who was far too demanding and lacked manners, despite his obvious wealth. The man didn't understand how gentlemen did business in the south. Just because Herschel liked to wear white linen suits didn't mean that he didn't get his hands dirty from time to time.

Herschel knew where most of the dirt was hidden in New Orleans. He knew many of the brothels, some of the dangerous criminals who remained at large, and all the illegal gambling joints operating in the area and surrounding parishes. He also knew who to ask for help when he needed it. The coroner was a good friend who frequently dined with Herschel. They went way back when Herschel was still an assistant DA. The case of fine wine he received every Christmas helped keep their relationship solid.

"I think the lady you are interested in came in as a Jane Doe. The report indicates she had dyed blond hair with traces of red as well. We used to call them strawberry blonds. She was about thirty years old, maybe a few years older. There was evidence of an earlier abortion. Apparent death was from a drug overdose, but no signs that she was a junkie. She was found naked in a bad section of town where the only white women are usually prostitutes. Hard to tell if she was one, or wasn't."

The coroner gave this brief report over the phone, reading from a file. He was too busy to meet for lunch. The woman was found about six months earlier and was never identified. She didn't have a police record. The body was held for the required time period. When it wasn't picked up, it was buried with all the other poor unknown souls nobody wanted to acknowledge. It was a growing problem with all the homeless people migrating to New Orleans. Jane Doe was now just another number.

Herschel was able to confirm Barry's earlier trip to New Orleans. Barry arrived on a Southwest flight on Wednesday evening and left the following afternoon. For someone who was supposedly searching for a missing wife, he certainly didn't stay long.

The private investigator Barry hired, Harold Davis, was a well-known lush who had difficulty finding his own office. The man was pitiful and Herschel wondered why anyone would associate with the man, much less hire him to find someone. Unless, you didn't want that person found and you were just going through the motions. In that case, Harold was a perfect selection.

Herschel wondered how Barry could have learned about Harold Davis. The man certainly didn't advertise, except for the sign in the window of his storefront office. Harold spent his mornings hanging around the halls of the courthouse hoping to pick up a client in need of help. Most potential clients took a pass once they observed the rumpled clothes, stained tie and smelled his whiskey-laden breath. Harold's specialty involved infidelity. He loved to peek into the personal affairs of others, particularly when they were cheating on their spouse. Yet the guards always said hello to him and pointed out the ones that might need an investigator. When he did click with one, he always passed out a meager finder's fee to the helpful guard. It was something that was practiced in most court houses, usually by lawyers.

Twenty years ago, at the age of 50, Herschel stopped driving. He felt maintaining an automobile in New Orleans was a wasted expense. Herschel's office was just one block from the famous St. Charles Avenue so he could easily ride the streetcar when it suited him. Other times, he took a taxi. Eventually he found a taxi driver named Dooley. Dooley had good perception, knew how to draw people out, learn interesting things about them while driving. Sometimes he'd share that information with Herschel.

It was inevitable that Dooley would become Herschel's personal part-time chauffer whenever Herschel needed transportation. He always gave Dooley his planned itinerary so Dooley knew when to show up without being called. Sometimes Dooley would just show up to impart some interesting tidbit. Other times Herschel would summon Dooley to obtain a bit of needed information.

Over the years, Dooley was often used when someone had to be discreetly followed. Dooley loved that kind of work. He knew the city and all the surrounding parishes so well that he could blend in with the traffic, never being spotted. Through him, Herschel had access to a network of taxi drivers who could report on where they'd taken a certain fare, or picked up a certain individual. This underground information network was essential for the kind of work Herschel was involved with.

It was through this informal taxi network that Herschel had confirmed whom Barry Greene had visited on his last trip to New Orleans. He'd been dropped off in front of Harold Davis's storefront office, taken there directly from the airport, so Barry had to know [Internet] of Harold Davis in advance.

Herschel was able to learn that Reggie was a local pimp, loan shark and part-time drug dealer with a reputation for violence. He wasn't a man you wanted to owe any money. How it was that Barry ever happened onto the man was anyone's guess. It would be almost impossible to interview Reggie, much less locate him. The man was constantly moving around on the street, in a protected neighborhood. Ask about Reggie's whereabouts and he'd know about it quickly.

Through Dooley, Herschel learned the rumor that Reggie also ran a place in a very undesirable section. If the Jane Doe died of a drug overdose, and her body was found in the vicinity of Reggie's activity, it could be reasonably speculated that Reggie had something to do with it. The man did a cash business, so it was difficult to believe that anyone would *owe him* anything. If anyone did, it would be wise to pay him promptly, to maintain one's health and continued well-being.

Herschel decided that Reggie needed to be located and watched. He enlisted Dooley's help for the assignment. One of the taxi drivers in the network would know where Reggie could be found.

It also appeared that Liz Miller was dead. Killed by a local drug dealer, who just happened to send an email message to Barry, stating that he was *owed* something. With Liz out of the way, the possibility of blackmail was eliminated… temporarily. It all depended on how much this Reggie character knew about Barry Greene and his precarious situation. Herschel wondered how someone like Barry Greene, not from New Orleans, would ever run into the likes of Reggie? Reggie didn't advertise in the yellow pages, an expense that continually annoyed Herschel.

Out of curiosity, Herschel called another private contact who knew someone in military records. After waiting a day, he learned that a Reggie Burgoins had been dishonorably discharged from the U. S. Army in 1992. He'd been caught stealing and selling military supplies. Checking further, Herschel was able to gather one more piece of useful information.

Private First Class Barry Greene was also in that same supply company, and therefore, probably knew Reggie. There was the connection.

Perhaps they kept in touch. If so, Barry might have a dark side yet to be discovered. Nick Alexander would be very pleased with this report and Herschel would continue to check out the mysterious Reggie. He found such assignments a real challenge and a nice diversion from his other cases. Plus, he'd become fond of Nick. He sensed the mutual respect they had for one another.

At 70, it was all Herschel lived for, having an excuse to call on old acquaintances for some small favor and to catch up on some local gossip, as well as to indulge in fine dining of course. It helped when he had a client picking up the tab.

Chapter 19

Reggie Burgoins enjoyed a bad reputation and took particular pleasure in that. Upon his release from a federal prison, he'd headed straight back home to New Orleans. Because of his dishonorable discharge, he couldn't get a decent job, not that he wanted one. He made a promise to himself that he'd never spend any more time behind bars... ever! He was aware that there were temporary muscle jobs he could do, and that was a start.

    He could remember collecting bad debts for a loan shark who called himself Willie. Reggie kept a percentage of what he collected, despite the old man's complaints. In time he took over the old man's accounts, cutting him out of the picture entirely. A few weeks later, Reggie was visited by another leg-breaker, not unlike himself. The man was much bigger than Reggie and presented a formidable shape standing in the doorway, Reggie recalled. The man tried to scare Reggie into leaving town, or get all his bones broken.

    Reggie had backed away pretending to be scared. When the man smiled and advanced on Reggie, he got half way across the room when Reggie put a hole in his head with a Colt 38 Police Special. The body turned up a few days later in a nearby dumpster. After that, no one bothered him, including the police. Willie never again tried to scare Reggie, and Reggie's reputation began to spread. After that incident, he was known as someone you didn't mess with. In an unplanned way, Willie actually enhanced Reggie's reputation as, "a bad coonass", a Cajun expression with several interpretations, none good.

Reggie already knew that to lend money to losers, he had to hang around the low-class bars. To kill time, he flirted with the local whores. They all knew him and his growing reputation. Because he was known to be dangerous, it also gave him an element of status and added to his sex appeal. As a consequence, he got all the free sex he wanted. Eventually, he offered some of the whores, those without pimps, his personal protection. Just like the loan sharking, he eased into becoming a part-time pimp. Even the local bartenders agreed, it was a natural transition.

The whores worked the streets and local bars while Reggie kept a close watch and counted the money. He made sure the bartenders were taken care of. That way, he always knew in advance who was looking for him and why. Reggie was generous with his informants. He knew it was necessary for survival. Money and sex were two commodities easily traded, easy to acquire and easy to get killed over, he frequently mused.

To keep his whores happy, and in line, Reggie kept a supply of coke. Over time he also developed regular customers who depended on him to supply their needs as well. His enterprise kept growing, yet it was all connected. He had to be careful to stay below the radar of the police, and the mob. That meant not getting too big, or too well known. He had to remain confined to a small concentrated ten-block area. There were other sections of town where he knew better than to show his face, regardless of his reputation.

One of his favorite bartenders gave him an alert that a known gang member was asking about him, "He's riding in a white Tahoe with those fancy spinning chrome wheels."

"He white, or black?" Reggie asked on his cell phone.

"He be white, but has an eye for the black whores."

"Uh huh, he alone, or somebody with him?"

"Somebody else is doing the driving. He didn't come in, stayed in the Tahoe."

Smart move, Reggie thought as he began forming his plan. He grabbed one of his younger girls and took her with him in search of the white Tahoe that was no doubt still cruising the neighborhood. He let her out on a corner where she'd be easy to spot. He gave her instructions what she was to do when they stopped, as they surely would.

His plan worked. The white Tahoe with the two white guys stopped when they spotted her smiling and giving them a shy wave. She looked to be about 17, but she was actually closer to 24 with lots of experience. She jumped into the Tahoe, sitting on the passenger's lap.

"Gee, it's kinda tight in the front seat, I think I'd prefer being in the back," she said giggling, as she crawled into the rear seat. She gave the driver instructions on how to get to a secluded spot, where the police wouldn't bother them. It was a dark alley that ran behind a row of two-story houses. Each house had a garage that opened onto the alley, sharing space with a variety of garbage cans and discarded trash.

"So, is Reggie your pimp?" The driver asked, running down the window and turning off the engine, but leaving the radio playing at low volume. It was a Ricky Martin CD pounding out a Latin beat. He was tapping the wheel to the rhythm and nodding his head.

"Uh huh. You guys know Reggie?"

"Yeah, you could say that. We're looking for him. You know where he is?"

"Well I know where he'll be in about a half hour from now."

"That's good, we can wait right here and you can entertain us while we're waiting. When we're done with you, you can take us to him," the passenger said getting out and getting into the back seat to join her.

"Honey, I don't mind doing both of you, but it ain't going to be a freebee, you understand?"

"Don't worry about it, we'll give the money directly to Reggie when we see him. Maybe even tell him how good you were."

"I don't usually work that way...."

"Oh I think you will this time," the passenger said taking out a switchblade knife, flicking it open.

"Please. Don't hurt me. I'm just a working girl. If you guys know Reggie, then you know he can get real mean sometimes." She was supposed to act scared and try to hold out for money, even though she already knew it wasn't going to be that way.

"Like I said, don't worry about it. My friend here is going to make sure you do a real good job." He pushed the knife closer all the while unzipping his pants. "Hey Frank, why don't you walk down to the end of the alley and have a smoke. Check things out while I keep this little sweetie busy back here."

"Okay, but I may want some of that, too." The driver got out and walked down the alley, leaving the two in the back seat. As instructed earlier, the girl had put down both rear windows.

"You better make this good, girl, or you may not be breathing when we drop your ass off, understand?"

She didn't have to fake being scared. She nodded and proceeded to take off her blouse as slowly as she could with trembling hands.

his seat for more room.

With all the windows down and the music playing, Reggie was able to slide noiselessly up to the passenger side, reach in and slice the man's throat in one quick movement. The driver was at the end of the alley smoking a cigarette and checking his watch. Reggie crawled into the front passenger seat, staying low and beeped the horn to get the driver's attention. He could see the driver discard his cigarette and start walking back to the Tahoe, and his pending doom.

It was a half-hour past dusk and the alley was dark, dark enough that the occupants of the SUV couldn't be seen from the outside. Before the driver arrived, Reggie had the passenger's knife as well as the automatic pistol he was carrying. He gave the girl the dead man's wallet.

"You get to keep all the money," he whispered while he waited.

The driver didn't appear to be in any hurry, nor was he acting cautious. As soon as he opened the door, Reggie stuck the dead man's automatic in his face.

"Get in. I understand you're looking for me," Reggie said.

The driver looked over the seat and saw his partner slumped over in the back seat, blood covering his shirt.

"You've just made a big mistake, sport. You got any idea who you're dealing with?"

"Consider that my question to you, now drive this thing to the end of the alley. I'll tell you when to stop."

"You're as good as dead already and you don't know it yet," the driver said, trying to act brave.

"Hell of an echo in here, I'm hearing you speak my words. Stop here." Reggie pushed the gun into the man's ribs. Sugar, get out and open that garage door for me."

"You won't get away with this," the driver grunted.

"Won't be anything you got to worry about. You answer the questions, I may let you live. You don't answer, you die, like your partner, who's still bleeding out as we speak."

"What do you want to know?"

"Just tell me the real reason you're so interested in Reggie, and who sent you?"

"You mean you can't guess?"

"A confirmation is always nice. And I need to know here to send the body parts."

"Screw you. You're planning on killing me anyway."

"That's true, but there are different ways of doing it. Your friend got it quick, you won't be that lucky. I'll take off a finger, one at a time."

The girl opened a garage door opposite where the SUV sat, while Reggie pushed him inside, gagged him with a dirty handkerchief, and closed the door. It would be enough to muffle the man's screams, as Reggie cut off a thumb. With that, the driver told Reggie everything he wanted to know. Reggie cut his throat and left him lying on the dirt floor to bleed out. He wrapped up the thumb in the man's handkerchief, which he'd deliver later.

Both bodies were stripped and thrown into the back of the vehicle, not worrying about any remaining blood. Reggie drove back to The Lodge where he gave his girl the rest of the night off, before proceeding out to one of his favorite fishing spots, a bayou about 20 miles away. The bodies would disappear in that murky water, making a great snack for the gators he'd seen lurking there. He planned to leave the Tahoe in a Wal-Mart parking lot with the engine running. He guessed it would take, at the most, five minutes before kids would be riding. Reggie removed the guns, the clothes and all the identifying paperwork in the glove box. He'd see that the thumb was delivered the next day. It was his way of sending a returned message. He knew it also made him an instant target, if he ever ventured outside his immediate neighborhood.

For the last five years, Reggie had been lending money at high interest rates, collecting all his own debts, supplying coke to a select number of special clients and providing sexy women to those who sought their services. The local cops were taken care of in various ways, depending on their needs, thus maintaining a secure position within the local neighborhood. Reggie began transitioning to younger women, cutting the older ones loose, to work the streets on their own, provided they worked in a different area. Some of the women were reluctant to leave. They feared and loved Reggie. For some, he was their only family.

Monique was his oldest lady. She was 42 and had a breast enhancement that she proudly exhibited.. Her trademark was a gold-capped front tooth that she displayed every time she smiled. She also wore a gold trimmed elastic G-string under her mini-skirt which she openly displayed to prospective johns.

Her regular johns knew her routine; she offered a *golden* opportunity... however you wanted it. Sitting on a bar stool, Monique would turn toward a prospective john, hike up her skirt and smile at the same time, making sure he got the full view, top and bottom. She was never subtle and didn't believe in wasting time.

Monique adored Reggie and was extremely jealous whenever Reggie showed any undo interest in any of the other ladies in his stable.

"Baby, you don't need to be messin' with anyone but me," she said frequently. "You know I'm always ready and available for you. I can still do things them young girls never even thought of." She told everyone she invented the original lap dance.

As wild as she was at times, Reggie grew bored. Younger, inexperienced girls drew his attention. The less attention he paid to Monique, the more she turned to drugs in frustration. It was the beginning of a downhill slide and

Reggie recognized the signs. In time Monique would have to go, just like the other older ladies. Turn over was part of the flesh game. He had to keep his regular clients happy and supply new bodies periodically for the sake of variety.

The problem was, Monique steadily turned a dozen tricks a night, and sometimes more. For Reggie, that was good income. She knew how to work a bar and the street. She jumped in and out of parked cars all night into the early hours of the morning. She gave the term, *working girl* real meaning. She frequently ended her night at a local all-night diner where she'd meet two local cops she knew and serviced regularly. Sometimes they'd give her a ride home after a brief delay in a darkened parking lot along the way. It was the cops who gave her the nickname, "Goldie".

One night, one of the cops, a few years younger than she, asked, "Why don't you stop this shit and marry me, Goldie?" It was his way of kidding her.

"Baby, you couldn't keep me happy. Sides, I like the variety. You'd have to be my pimp, on account there ain't no one man could ever keep me satisfied." Then she laughed so loud it startled both cops. They knew she was high. That also made her unpredictable.

"I could handle that," one cop said straightening his uniform.

"And I don't do no cookin', no laundry and no cleanin'," she added.

"Hell, I guess it's not much different from what I got now," he replied with a chuckle.

As his business continued to prosper, Reggie bought an old house that survived several bad storms, but had some damage. He was able to buy it cheap. Earlier, it had been converted into an apartment building. It was three stories high, had six apartments and needed considerable repairs. He named it "The Lodge" and spent a fortune refurbishing the interior, using one of the first floor units as his office and private suite. The small brass sign above the entrance read:

The Lodge for Wayward Souls

People passing by on the sidewalk thought it was a religious retreat, or an orphanage.

The ladies took their tricks into the other first floor unit across the hallway. That way Reggie could keep a close watch on the activity coming in and going. He also had a one-way mirror that allowed him to keep tabs on the activity. He rarely had a problem. When some perverted drunk started to beat on one of the ladies, Reggie was quick to the rescue.

He had a special talent for restraining rough clients. Once subdued, Reggie made the offender strip naked and forced them to "bow before the offended princess". That translated to the John being on his knees, his head between the girl's thighs, giving pleasure, and asking for forgiveness, to the one he'd bruised.

All the while Reggie was using a Polaroid camera to advantage. He'd take the man's wallet, remove any money that was left, jot down the person's name and address from his driver's license and note any other useful information. It served as a good insurance policy against any reprisals later.

A cab was always waiting nearby to haul the jerk away to another area of the city. The offenders were reminded to never stop back, for any reason. Reggie made a point of protecting his whores. Over time he acquired quite a collection of photos and gave some serious thought about going into the porno trade.

Reggie left the shabby exterior of the brick building untouched, to blend in with the rest of the decaying neighborhood. It was situated in the middle of a sixteen square block area he controlled. The women were not allowed to stray outside that area for any reason without his permission. All his whores lived upstairs when they weren't working. This way he had complete control and knew when they were sick.

Some of the drivers, in the same taxi network Herschel utilized, were also a good resource for Reggie. He got business from out of town visitors looking for the services his girls provided. Any cab driver who brought a client was treated to something to eat while he waited, plus he was given a small monetary reward. It was a lot less expensive than advertising escorts in the yellow pages, something Reggie refused to do. He only accepted phone calls from those he knew, never from strangers.

Over time Reggie became computer literate, bought a computer and kept disguised records. He flirted with young women and girls over the Internet. Whores wore out just like used cars and trucks. In time they needed to be replaced. Only Monique remained. The Internet provided him with a vast number of young prospects.

Girls thinking about running away were lured to New Orleans where Reggie would meet them at the bus station, offering them a place to stay at The Lodge, where they could train for a new career, if it appealed to them. If not, they were free to leave. Reggie never felt the need to hold anyone against their wishes. He always enjoyed the interview process where he determined if they were suitable candidates. Most weren't, and he sent them on their way to one of the many strip clubs in the city. Like Reggie, the clubs were always looking for young fresh flesh. Because he was a good resource, Reggie managed to survive the mob's influence. They indulged him as a minor nuisance and warned him about expansion. "Don't even think about it," he was told.

Reggie made it a point to never suggest to anyone, over the Internet, that they leave home. That was always the girl's decision. If they decided they wanted to visit New Orleans, then he was available to, "help them out temporarily with a place to stay". As a result, he got more candidates than he needed, so he was able to pick and chose the best. Every interview involved a sexual encounter, to see if the candidate was creative and willing to perform a variety of sexual acts. If not, the interview was terminated at once. Reggie never forced himself on anyone. It had to be voluntary, which was part of the screening process. Most were too shy to volunteer to do anything, including taking off their clothes.

It was just a matter of time before Reggie became bored. The loan sharking and pimping were routine. Collecting a debt wasn't a problem because Reggie's reputation was enough to scare anyone. He decided he needed a hobby, something he could feel passionate about. He had a cousin who was a chef at one of the better restaurants in the French Quarter. Reggie's cousin, in exchange for some sexual favors from the ladies, agreed to teach Reggie the finer culinary arts. He also agreed to help redesign the kitchen into a gourmet's delight.

As a result, all the ladies at The Lodge looked forward to dinner each night before embarking to their respective zones. They would sit around a huge round table in the dining area and discuss their respective misadventures. It was a family-type atmosphere that Reggie had unwittingly created. What he desperately needed was a mature woman to be the madam of The Lodge; to keep the whores in line and also tend to their special needs; getting them examinations.

Monique seemed like a good candidate but she was too preoccupied with turning tricks. It was all she knew, all

Searching for Rachel

she wanted. And, she couldn't be completely trusted when she got high.

Reggie took in a young runaway black girl, Sophie who was 16 and looked closer to 12. She wore pigtails and a wide grin. She was skinny and she wanted to be a *whoor* like her older sister, but Reggie had other plans for her. He needed someone to keep the place clean and do all the laundry. Every day there were dozens of towels and sheets to be washed, floors to be mopped.

At times Reggie likened his situation to that of a motel owner. Sophie soon learned the trade by being a casual observer, when she wasn't busy in the laundry. After a few weeks at The Lodge, Sophie put on some needed pounds. When she arrived, she was rail thin with all her bones showing. Working in the kitchen with Reggie, she learned how to snack. She kept the kitchen spotless and quickly became a maid and cook's assistant.

One day Reggie received an email message from an old army buddy, Barry Greene. Barry was selling cars in Nashville and thinking about taking a few days off, to visit New Orleans. He was hoping to get together with Reggie.

When he arrived, Reggie made sure Barry had plenty of female attention. He gave Barry a very detailed tour of New Orleans. They explored all the tourist joints in the French Quarter taking along two young women as escorts, causing a lot of heads to turn and stare. When Monique learned that she wasn't going with them, she threw a fit and left in a rage.

"It was the best short vacation" Barry could ever remember taking, he told his friend. Reggie made sure his friend was kept well-fed and well-serviced. Sophie even washed his back while Barry sat in an old-style, claw-foot bathtub on the third floor. The room he was in had a great view and a balcony overlooking a small courtyard in the back of the house. When the girls weren't busy, they'd stop by to see him, teasing him. They thought he had a cute accent, and they also thought Tennessee was in another part of the world.

After that trip, Barry and Reggie kept in touch using the Internet. Reggie was a resource Barry might use someday. After all, Barry was the only one who knew the true facts about the mysterious death of an army supply sergeant who'd threatened to expose Reggie. If Barry had ever revealed those facts, Reggie would still be living the rest of his life in Leavenworth prison. Because of that deadly secret, Barry knew he could always trust Reggie. However, neither of them ever mentioned it.

A year later, Reggie got Barry's wedding announcement and was tempted to attend the wedding, but decided he didn't want to leave New Orleans, even for just a few days. Too many bad things could happen when he wasn't watching his enterprise closely. The whores could get hurt, or hold back on him. His operation required constant supervision. He was glad to hear that Barry had married well.

They no longer had anything in common, except a few past army experiences. Never the less, they continued to keep in touch as friends. Like Barry, Reggie didn't have many close friends, people he could trust with a secret. Having Barry visit was a nice change and he'd enjoyed the time they spent together, even though Barry spent a lot of time in his room on the third floor with the girls.

And then, seven years later, Barry needed a big favor.

Chapter 20

Ezra Rueben wanted an update from Nick. Nick tried to give him a brief synopsis of his trips to New Orleans and Ocala. Much as he hated to do it, he was compelled to relate the details about Liz, but not mentioning that she looked a lot like Rachel.

"So, Barry wasn't playing golf on Wednesdays after all. He was screwing around on Rachel!" Ezra was trying to remain calm.

It annoyed him that he didn't know about Barry's infidelity earlier. He might have used that to some advantage. It was still an important item, in that it helped to establish a possible motive, which until now had been missing.

"Yes, I think we can pretty much conclude Barry had a girlfriend on the side. And it looks like she may have helped him establish an alibi, if that was Liz who was seen leaving the houseboat and driving away in Rachel's convertible."

"Which means Rachel could have been killed someplace else and earlier that weekend, when Barry wouldn't have had a suitable alibi," Ezra said. He was following Nick's line of reasoning and anticipating a conclusion.

"The problem is, we don't know when that might have happened, or where. I think Barry used New Orleans as a red herring to throw the investigation in that direction, knowing he couldn't possibly remain a suspect for long."

"That smug bastard! We have to find Rachel's body."

"Yes, and I'm working on that. Establishing the exact time of death will be extremely difficult now, even after we find the body. So much time has elapsed. You can bet he'll never confess to anything," Nick said.

"I guess I underestimated him. He knew I was watching him closely and yet he had the nerve to cheat on Rachel, making a fool out of the family. I should think that would be sufficient grounds for gaining custody of Jonathan."

"Just wait. We don't want to tip our hand just yet about what we know and what we think may have happened." Nick was working on a plan to scare Barry, or at least to worry him enough to make a mistake.

Nick had Herschel send an email message to Barry using Reggie's email address. Herschel had to enlist the services of a local hacker who was a college student to accomplish this. The message he sent read:

> Hey old buddy, just a quick heads up to be very careful. The police were here asking a lot of questions. I'm being watched, so it's best for now if you don't contact me. I'm going to take a quick vacation and get lost. Stay cool.
>
> Reggie

Herschel Fielding liked the way Nick worked. It was evidence of years of experience, and it was easy to respect that. Barry would no doubt start to worry, once he read the message and realized that the police had made some sort of connection with Reggie. It served as a reminder the case was still active and progress was being made. As a former prosecuting attorney, Herschel knew that when a suspect was nervous, they often made mistakes.

Herschel's driver, Dooley had an address for The Lodge, having deposited a few visitors there. Herschel was developing a plan to unsettle Reggie.

Liz Miller remembered she had been very upset about the way Barry had suddenly summoned her. He'd told her he wanted to spend the weekend with her on his father-in-law's houseboat on Center Hill Lake. He'd said he'd recently learned his wife was cheating on him and had given him some flimsy excuse, leaving him alone for the weekend. Barry didn't want anyone to know that she'd left. He wanted Liz to pretend she was Rachel, just for the weekend. In return, Barry had a big surprise for her. He was sending her to New Orleans for a week and also promised to pay her $15,000 just to be an actress for a few days.

Barry gave her $5,000 when she arrived and said he'd give her the rest when she returned from New Orleans. No one was to know anything about the plan. She was to fly down to New Orleans on Sunday afternoon using his wife's credit card. She'd fly back later on a different carrier and pay cash for that return ticket. Going down, she would be a redhead. Coming back she could be a blonde once again.

Liz thought it was a hastily conceived plan but was intrigued enough to go along with it. The money was important. She needed some new furniture and a better car. Her ancient Honda Civic needed some major repair work done soon and she couldn't afford it. She liked Barry, and the prospect of seeing New Orleans for a week was exciting, even though it was close to her old stamping grounds.

Before meeting Barry, she'd done a quick dye job on her hair, which he'd asked her to do, and it turned out pretty well, she had to admit. Looking into the mirror, she told herself she was auditioning to be an actress for the weekend and she was close to the truth. She did wonder why Barry's wife had left her Mercedes convertible at home and how was it that Barry had her credit card? If, for some reason Barry got caught, it would be his problem, not hers, she reminded herself.

Liz remembered having a problem finding the remote spot where she was to meet Barry. At one time it had been a public boat launching area that was now closed. Barry told her the gate would be unlocked. She didn't know that Barry had used bolt cutters on the lock then replaced it with another, leaving the gate unlocked for her. Later, he'd relock the gate and have a key to enter when he wanted to, so she could retrieve her car. That's what he told her and she didn't have any reason then to suspect anything different.

Barry had met her at the remote spot, driving a red Mercedes convertible. Together, they drove to the marina. All weekend long he had her practice signing his wife's name. He gave her detailed instructions on what he wanted her to do once she left the houseboat. And for once, he wasn't all that horny. That surprised her. She'd never seen Barry act so nervous. At times he was distracted, repeating himself, as if trying to make sure he didn't overlook something. His changed demeanor made Liz nervous.

New Orleans turned out to be a surprise. Liz wasn't prepared for Reggie. She was expecting some sleazy low life-type who would smell bad and be all over her as soon as they were alone in the car. Instead, she was met by a good-looking man, about Barry's age, with dark brown wavy hair, and a very engaging smile. His teeth appeared to be perfect. His nails were manicured. And while he was dressed casually, she could tell the clothes were expensive. He was wearing alligator loafers and no socks, the new style for being hip, she thought.

There had been a cab waiting for them just outside the baggage pickup area. The driver took her bags and seemed exceptionally courteous. He also called Reggie by his first name. Reggie never told him where they were going, the driver already knew. It was like being chauffeured, only it was in a very clean taxi, instead of a limo.

Liz had no idea what was in store next, but she was excited never the less. Reggie explained that he and Barry had been friends for many years.

Chapter 21

Reggie Burgoins was used to being around attractive, sexy women. After all, he was in the flesh business. When he first saw Liz, he was perplexed why Barry would ask him to get rid of her? She was a beauty. And later, he learned that she was also very intelligent. She knew a little about Reggie, but not a lot.

Reggie turned on the old charm, took Liz back to The Lodge where he had a separate room waiting for her. It was the same room Barry had stayed in years before. Sophie had fresh flowers in a vase beside the bed. The room was spotless and comfortable. This, too, was a total surprise since the exterior of the building was a sharp contrast to the interior. Reggie explained it was a whorehouse and found it interesting that she didn't appear to be the least bit shocked, mildly surprised maybe.

Liz met all the ladies and instantly sensed a dislike from Monique. She wondered if she was emitting a similar signal. Invisible sparks flew across the room. Liz wondered if this was perhaps Reggie's private squeeze. The woman certainly acted like a jealous wife.

On Monday, Reggie took Liz shopping for some needed items then they did some people watching and sight seeing. Liz explained she was originally from the Baton Rouge area, but had no desire to return there.

Searching for Rachel

Later on Monday evening, after grocery shopping, Reggie explained his entire operation to Liz. She was instantly impressed with his enterprise and his expertise. She confided that she'd once been a working girl herself and thought Reggie's girls had it made compared to what she'd had to put up with. Reggie cooked a late dinner and they stayed up late talking openly about their respective pasts. They also finished off two bottles of wine.

Liz found herself taken with Reggie and hoped that Barry wouldn't bother flying down later, as he'd promised to do. He could just mail the rest of the money. She would be content to remain a while longer, if not indefinitely. She knew Reggie and Barry were friends, yet it surprised her that Reggie was so open and frank about what he was doing. He seemed to be putting an exceptional amount of trust in her, telling her confidential information about himself and his business. She kept wondering why?.

She recalled there was no lock on her bedroom door and she half expected Reggie to join her later that night. She was a little disappointed when he didn't.

The next morning Reggie had a sumptuous breakfast waiting. Sophie did all the serving and removed all the dirty dishes. After everyone had left the room, and over a third cup of strong coffee, Reggie revealed the rest of Barry's plan to her. She wasn't supposed to return to Nashville! She was supposed to die of a drug overdose, while in New Orleans. *No wonder he felt so sure of himself, telling me all that confidential information. He knew I wouldn't be around to tell anyone,* she had thought.

Her anger was instant. Liz realized for the first time that Barry had tricked her. And, he'd cheated her out of $10,000 he still owed her. She realized she'd never collect it now. And, the bastard had arranged for her to be murdered. What else was he capable of? She hadn't seen any newspapers, or watched any television news and wasn't aware of Rachel's disappearance. She'd been too busy enjoying herself. It was, after all, the first time that a man had shown so much interest and been so gallant.

Reading her thoughts, Reggie went on to explain the plan he'd thought of during the night. While Liz was sleeping, Reggie was considering his options. No way was he going to kill this woman, even for his pal, Barry. Liz was just the person he'd wanted, to supervise his enterprise. She'd be the perfect madam. She had the right background and he felt he could trust her. In fact, she was the first person to ever gain his trust. He'd told her things about himself that he'd never mentioned to anyone before.

Reggie also knew that Monique would be a problem once Liz became the new boss. He'd deal with that problem soon enough. Monique was overdue to go any way, regardless of how much money she brought in.

Reggie made his proposal. Liz would have her own suite at The Lodge. She'd run the ladies for him, keeping everyone in line, which would free him to do other things, even take a trip perhaps, without having to worry. He explained that while Barry wanted her wasted, he had no intention of following through on that. Nor did he plan to tell Barry she was still alive. He had to call Barry collect later, from a pay phone, at the bus station as instructed.

It annoyed Reggie that Barry had cheated Liz out of all that money. If he could do that to Liz, then what else was he capable of? Based on what Liz had told him, he was fairly certain Barry had killed his wife. No doubt he planed to collect some insurance money later. And perhaps at that time, whenever that was, Reggie might remind Barry, that he still owed Liz $10,000, plus some healthy interest. Reggie would be the collector and Barry would learn, much to his surprise, that Liz was still alive. No doubt it would be the end of their friendship as well. For now, he'd lie and tell Barry, "everything had been taken care of"'. That would buy him some time.

Two months passed and Reggie was relieved to learn that Barry had moved to Ocala. He also learned that Barry was suspected of killing his wife, according to news reports. That meant that he and Liz were the only people who could put Barry at risk with the police. So now, each man had something to hold over the other. It was a good and fortuitous trade-off. Neither could reveal anything about what they knew about the other. It was a good Cajun stand-off.

Months later, a huge fat man in a white linen suit appeared at The Lodge. He was leaning on a cane. A taxi was waiting at the curb.

Chapter 22

Barry Greene was worried about the private investigator, the one who showed up at his front door and pushed his way inside, without being invited. The guy knew about Liz! Keith must have spilled the beans. It was the only way the guy could have known about her. Unless... Ezra had someone following him when he was in Nashville. He wouldn't put it past the old bastard. But why hadn't he thrown it in his face? It was something Ezra would take pleasure in doing.

Barry also worried about Reggie. If he was arrested by the police, or his place was raided, there was always that remote possibility Reggie might try to make a deal using Barry's plight as a bargaining chip. While Reggie didn't know the whole story, he was capable of putting some of the pieces together and drawing a conclusion that would interest the police. Barry still owed Reggie for making Liz disappear. Like it, or not, he had to trust his friend ... for a while longer.

He felt certain that once Reggie met Liz, he would have second thoughts about making her disappear and try to use her as one of his street whores. Barry hoped that Reggie would see the danger that posed. Liz didn't know the whole story either, but she knew enough, and like

Reggie, could cause him a lot of trouble. If Liz were still alive, she could, and would, shake him down for a bundle. Barry harked back to an old anecdote his father used to say. "If two people know a secret, in time it will not be a secret." Two other people knew parts of Barry's secret and he was definitely worried.

It was the early part of Happy Hour at Harry's and Barry was deep in thought, watching CNN, but not actually aware of what was being said, or shown. He was so preoccupied he hadn't noticed the lady who sat down next to him at the bar. He smelled her perfume and turned. He recognized the attractive lady sitting next to him. It was Amanda McBride.

"I think I've seen you in here before," she said, pretending not to recognize him.

"Yes, you have. And I've noticed you, too. It's Amanda isn't it?"

"Aha, so you did know who I was. How have you been?"

"Okay. I've been meaning to call you ...."

"Oh, and you lost my card, right?"

"No, actually I still have your card. It's on my desk at work."

"Well now you don't have to bother calling, I'm right here. Excuse me a moment." She gave the bartender a drink order and turned back to Barry. "Okay, what kind of trip were you thinking about?" *If he still had her card, it had to be her travel cover.*

Careful now, he reminded himself. *Don't rush this. This was a worldly woman who no doubt had heard all the greatest pick-up lines.*

"Let me pose a hypothetical question." *God she was gorgeous,* he thought, trying to stay on track with so many things running through his head. She was obviously single and obviously interested, since she'd sat down next to him at the bar, knowing at least a little about him. "If someone, say an American citizen, wanted to go somewhere outside the country and become a fugitive, where would be the best place for him, or her, to visit for a long-term stay?"

"First of all, I'd want payment in advance," she said laughing. She took a sip of her drink and contemplated the question for a minute. "I'd probably suggest Belize. They don't have an extradition agreement with us. And, it's a good, inexpensive place to be in exile." *Was he thinking about leaving the country?*

"Good, I'll have to keep that in mind, next time I rob a bank."

"I hope you're not serious. I was just trying to give you an honest answer. These days, it's difficult to hide anywhere, if the right people are looking for you. The new bounty hunters can track anyone, anywhere. Of course there has to be a strong reason, and a lot of money involved."

"You sound like you've had some experience in this exile and fugitive thing."

"No, not really. I do happen to know a guy who hires out, to track people, and he told me a little about it."

"If I decided to go, say for just a short trip, like a long weekend, would you go with me?" He hadn't meant for it to come out like that.

"Gee, I don't know, you haven't even bought me a drink yet." Again she laughed.

"Hey I apologize. I guess I'm not my normal self today. That was stupid on my part. I was trying to make small talk and I'm, well I'm not very good at it, as you can see."

"Would you like me to send you some information about Belize?"

"No, that's alright. It was more like a fantasy idea."

"What, robbing a bank?"

"No, no, going someplace where nobody knew who you were, and didn't care where you were from."

"Huh, I think you can save some money. We've got some lower-class joints right here in Ocala that would fit that requirement."

"My turn to ask, how would such a lovely woman like you know about those places?"

"Oh, you'd be surprised the places I've been, but we won't go there?" *Careful.* "So how's the real estate business, selling any houses?" She had to change the subject, fast.

"It's amazing how many retirees drop by the office and want to look at everything. It can wear you out."

"Like they say, if you don't do it, somebody else will." Amanda dropped some money on the bar. "Catch you later, Barry."

She remembered his name. That was a point in his favor. And, she indicated that she'd been around slumming in some of the seedy joints. Somehow that didn't seem to compute. She was too classy to go to any of those places. He wondered if she did drugs. That would at least explain a few things. He was tempted to follow her, see where she went, where she lived. Why not? Barry paid his bill and left hoping to get a glimpse of her and see what kind of wheels she had.

As luck should have it, Barry saw her backing out of an angled parking spot on the square. It was always difficult to find an open space there. Barry was parked on a side street, but he did see that she was driving a newer style Ford Mustang GT. It was silver and had a distinctive roar as she drove off. He liked her taste in cars.

When Barry arrived home, he took out the local phone book hoping to find Amanda McBride listed. She wasn't. He did, however, see a bold listing for McBride Investigations. How much of a coincidence was that, he wondered. He jotted down the address of the firm and told Jonathan they were going out to get something to eat.

"Daddy, you just drove past McDonalds," Jonathan complained. They passed several good fast food places already and he was hungry.

"We'll stop in a minute, son. I just need to check something out first."

Barry found the address. McBride Investigations was located in a renovated house. There was limited parking in front, but a much larger parking area in back. Passing by slowly, Barry was able to see a silver Mustang GT parked in back.

They're coming at me from all directions, he thought to himself. He was glad now that he'd decided to check out Amanda. As attractive as she was, he was glad he hadn't said too much to her. He was tempted to walk in the office now and say hello, just to let them know he was onto their game. If he had any doubts before, about being followed, he had none now. Maybe he should call her and ask her out, suggest going to one of those seedy places she knew. He wondered how far he could push it.

Amanda McBride left Barry sitting at the bar. She had to get back to the office and give her father a report on this latest bit of news.

"I think Barry might be considering leaving the country," she said. She went on to relate the entire brief conversation. "He tried to make a joke of it later, so maybe he realized that he'd tipped his hand a little more than he intended."

"Do you think he suspects you're a pee eye?" Charles asked.

"No, I didn't get that feeling. He's just sort of cautious. I caught him looking at the doorway a few times.

Searching for Rachel

I think he checks out people coming in, but does it casually. I had the feeling he was expecting someone, or he thinks someone is watching him. You'd better warn Gordon to be careful."

"We need to check and see if he has a passport, and if it's current. If not, he's not going anywhere for a few months," Charles said. He also had to consider whether or not to report this to Ezra Rueben. At least it was something new to report. During their last phone conversation, Charles told Ezra about Nick Alexander showing up. Ezra had alerted Charles that Nick was coming, so the visit wasn't a surprise. What did surprise him was Ezra spending so much money on investigators. The man seemed obsessed. *Good thing he's rich and can afford it,* he thought. Gordon's call interrupted his thoughts.

"Hey boss, I think our guy is wise to us. I caught him watching Amanda leave Harry's place. He got a good look at her Mustang. He didn't follow her. He picked up his kid, stopped by his condo for about ten minutes then drove past the office very slowly. I think he saw Amanda's Mustang parked out back."

"Shit. This is a new wrinkle we don't need. But better to know. Thanks, Gordon. Make sure he doesn't spot you. Hang way back."

Charles had been thinking about using Amanda to get closer to Barry, now that they'd made a casual connection, but not now. She'd have to keep her distance.

Barry Greene stopped for something to eat with Jonathan, then drove back to the condo, always watching his rearview mirror. He knew he'd brought his passport with him when he packed up for the move to Ocala, but he couldn't recall if it was current, or expired. A quick three-day trip to Belize City would make for a nice escape, even if it was just a short trip. It would give him time enough to scope out possibilities, maybe locate a bank where he could open an account. Finding a job might be a problem, unless he could sell real estate there to Americans wanting to retire out of the country. It was worth investigating. He'd use the Internet to learn as much as he could about the place. First, he had to find his passport.

Instead of parking in his usual spot, in front of his building, where he could see the Explorer from his front room windows, Barry thought of finding a different place, not so noticeable. He drove around the condo complex several times trying to decide on the best spot. He didn't care if it meant walking some extra steps. From now on, his routine would not be predictable. And, it was time to consider an alternative plan, in case Reggie gave him up. Reggie hadn't asked many questions, but the man was smart enough to put it all together. The one item that nobody else knew was where Rachel was. He alone knew that answer. She wouldn't be coming back anytime soon. Ezra could hire all the investigators he wanted, it would just be money wasted.

Chapter 23

Reggie Burgoins did everything possible to make Liz feel comfortable. He took her shopping for new clothes, bought some fancy jewelry and sent her out for a makeover with a hair stylist he knew. Unlike the rest of the girls, she was free to go wherever she wanted to go, just as long as he knew where she would be. He could insure her safety, as long as she remained at The Lodge, or in the immediate neighborhood, but not beyond.

He hoped, given time to adjust, she'd become his business partner. He knew there was a magnetic attraction that pulled both ways. When he thought about it, he had to admit it was an odd atmosphere for a romance to blossom, yet that's what was happening, despite the daily tantrums being made by Monique. Liz told Reggie the whore would have to leave soon and he agreed. The woman was causing too many distractions and was becoming a serious liability.

He'd have to dispose of her in the same way as he'd done earlier with the strawberry blond he picked up in the French Quarter He'd used her body as a decoy. He'd been looking for someone who generally resembled Liz, just in case the police should ever decide to look for her. He doubted that would happen. At any rate, there was a Jane Doe listed somewhere that would satisfy any inquiries.

The woman he'd picked up was looking to make a score and he was able to provide just what she needed. Once she was high, he added a booster. It was enough cocaine to put her into a coma. He then stripped off her clothes and made it look like she'd been raped. The police would regard her as just another unfortunate junkie/hooker. Reggie deliberated on whether or not to mention this to Liz. He was afraid of scaring her. He was trying to keep the violent aspects of his life to a minimum. The mob was leaving him alone, for the time being, and the cops weren't interested in his activity, except to partake in a few fleshy favors now and then.

To his way of thinking, the dead woman helped to provide Liz with a secure future. It could only get better, if she stuck with him. Monique could no longer be trusted, not that he ever had. He also knew he couldn't just turn her out. She'd go to the police out of revenge and there'd be an investigation that couldn't be prevented. Reggie didn't want any police attention. He knew about the two cops Monique serviced regularly. They frequently dropped her off late and knew about The Lodge. They'd be among the first asking about her.

Monique had to retire in a manner that coincided with her career, such as it was. Not too much would be made of the incident. Without discussing his plans with Liz, he took Monique out to do some shopping for new clothes. She was thrilled, thinking she'd have Reggie to herself for the entire afternoon, away from that new bitch, Liz. She'd been considering various ways to eliminate the competition and had already settled on poison.

It was just a matter of time. She had to be careful because Sophie watched her every move, whenever Monique was in the kitchen. It was like she was invading Sophie's territory. She could still remember telling her, "Look girl, you're nothing but a maid in a whorehouse.

I'm the one who brings in the money around here, not you. Just remember that next time you start getting upidy wid me."

Without suspecting anything unusual, time ran out for Monique. Her naked body was found in a dumpster, just like several others. Once again, it was a drug overdose. The police recognized her as one of the local working girls. Police were beginning to suspect they had a serial killer to deal with, someone who hated and abused whores.

When Reggie returned, he explained to Liz that Monique was no longer a problem. Alive she was a liability. Reggie didn't give Liz any of the details, nor did she ask. It scared her to think he could kill someone like it was just another business transaction and promptly forget it. On the other hand, it was also comforting to know that Reggie was trying to protect her.

When Sophie learned that Monique wasn't coming back, she immediately ran up to Monique's room, gathering up clothes, shoes and jewelry and offering the items to the other girls. To her surprise, nobody wanted any of it.

"It's tainted stuff, just like a curse. I wouldn't wear any of it if you paid me," one girl said.

"Store it all in the basement," Liz suggested. There would be other girls, later, who would be happy to have some of those things. For sure, they couldn't be thrown away.

It was a week before anyone came around to discuss Monique's disappearance. It was a detective Reggie had met a few times. He wasn't a customer.

"Look, I know about your establishment here," the detective said. They were sitting in the kitchen and Reggie had Sophie pour them coffee, the good stuff with a little brandy. "I also know that Monique worked for you."

"Okay. A lot of people know that," Reggie said.

"You didn't report her missing. How come?"

"Come on, get real. These girls come and go all the time. It's a revolving door. Your boss comes here regularly, but he doesn't want the same girl every time. You get what I'm saying?"

"Don't try to shine me, Reggie. Just because I don't take advantage of what you got going here, doesn't mean I'm stupid. I've asked around. Monique was with you a long time. People say she and you had a thing going. So how come you don't appear to be too concerned that she's gone?"

"People say a lot of crazy shit. That don't make it so. Monique wasn't my bed woman. She didn't sleep with me. She just made me some money. She also gave me a hard time."

"Oh? Care to explain that?"

"By that I mean, she was unpredictable. Acted crazy sometimes. You ask enough people around here, you'll find out I'm telling you the truth."

"So what'd you do, just dump her in a metal trash box to get rid of her?"

"Hey, that's cold, man. I've retired my share of whores and they're still working in other parts of town. Just ask around. I treat my ladies with a lot of respect. I don't have to kill anyone, unless they should threaten me in some way."

"You telling me you killed someone in the past, or did Monique pose a threat?"

"No, what I'm telling you is, I'm capable of taking care of business, any kind of business. Good, bad or otherwise. If, and I'm only saying if, someone was to make a threat against me, or my enterprise here, then I might take it upon myself to act, in a defensive manner, of course." Reggie said this with a wide grin. "I don't believe in violence," he added with a knowing smile.

"Uh huh. You expect me to believe your bullshit? If some of the higher ups knew about what you're up to, they'd shut you down in a heart beat."

"So how is it then they haven't done it? Ask yourself that question, and think about the answer, all the way back to your cubby hole of an office."

"We're not done yet, Reggie. When was the last time you saw Monique?"

"Must have been about a week ago. She had a couple favorite joints where she'd hang. Someone there could probably put a better time to what you're looking for."

"You have any arguments with her about then?"

"Hell, I had arguments with her every day she worked for me. She thought she was the Queen of Sheba."

"Any ideas on who might have done her?" The detective asked, finishing his coffee.

"No, and I don't think it was any of her regular johns. I'm guessing she got into a car with a stranger. And for her to do that, she musta been high. Not thinking clearly."

"I know a lot of people think, so what, because she was a whore. To me she was still a human being and didn't deserve to die that way," The detective said, heading for the door.

"So you think somebody killed her? Is that what you're saying?"

"Look, we don't know yet the exact cause of death, but it looks pretty obvious it was an overdose. She'd been doing drugs for a long time, according to the people I talked to, so you'd think she'd know better. And, she didn't just take off all her clothes and climb into a dumpster to take a nap. Somebody put her there."

"Have you considered that some homeless person might have stumbled upon her, took her stuff and threw her body in the box? I could see something like that happening. We got lots of homeless people around here."

"That's an interesting theory, but not one I'm going to try to sell to my boss. You see anyone walking around, wearing her stuff, give me a yell."

"I hate to say it, but it's one of the perils of being in the business," Reggie trying to wax philosophically.

"What, getting old, getting high or getting killed?"

That man knows more than he's letting on, Reggie thought. Sending him, instead of one of the people Reggie knew, was cause for a little concern. The mob wouldn't shed a tear if Reggie's enterprise was suddenly shut down. He had to keep that in mind and start preparing for the day when it was time to leave town. He'd probably take Liz with him, lock the door and not look back. Maybe start a gourmet restaurant somewhere over in Biloxi.

Searching for Rachel

Chapter 24

Herschel Fielding was unprepared for what happened when he knocked on the ornate door at The Lodge. The woman who opened the door was striking. It took a few seconds for her image to properly register.

He was looking at Rachel, or perhaps this was Liz. Her photo was etched into his brain and the recognition slipped out.

"Hello Liz, what a pleasant surprise!"

"I'm sorry, I don't believe we've ever met." She was in shock that this man knew her, had recognized her instantly. *Had Barry hired someone to find her?*

"Allow me to introduce myself. My name is Herschel Fielding." He presented his card and leaned on his cane, waiting for her to react, all the while watching her facial expressions.

"And how may I help you, Mr. ah, Fielding?"

"Perhaps we could sit down somewhere." He already knew about The Lodge being one of Reggie's establishments. He was surprised that he hadn't heard of it earlier, since he knew most of the established whorehouses in New Orleans. He'd been a patron of a few in his younger days when randy feelings still vibrated. Right now he wished he still had those type feelings. Instead, he'd have to settle for a cigar later.

With some trepidation, Liz invited the old gentleman inside. She guided him to the kitchen table and offered him a cup of coffee. Sophie served them and quickly left shooting Liz a curious look as she closed the door.

"I've been searching for you and Rachel Greene for quite some time. It seems you both disappeared about the same time in Tennessee, and the police have been baffled to say the least."

"First of all, my name isn't Liz, and I don't know any Rachel Greene. And how is it that you came here looking?"

"A private investigator has many sources. The police gave up on you when they discovered what they thought was your body discarded in a dumpster. I'm pleased to learn that it wasn't you." Herschel was sitting and leaning forward on his cane, never breaking eye contact.

"Well, I'm certainly glad that it wasn't me in that dumpster, too, but you're still mistaken. My name is, and always has been, Lucille. I'm from Baton Rouge, not Nashville." Liz realized her mistake the moment she mentioned *Nashville*. The man didn't seem to pick up on it and she held her breath.

Herschel did indeed pick up on the slip. He hadn't mentioned Nashville, yet the woman knew where the missing Liz was from. He also knew it was time to take his leave, while he still could. Reggie didn't seem to be around, for which he was grateful.

"Then I guess it's all a big mistake, Lucille. I'm truly sorry if I caused you any alarm. They say that we all have a double. If that's so, then somewhere in this crazy world, there's someone who must look a lot like me, poor devil. It happens all the time."

"Sophie will show you out," Liz said curtly. She didn't want to delay the man's departure. She was rattled and tried hard not to show it. Her hands were trembling and her legs were weak. She held onto the chair for support. If only Reggie were there, he'd know what to do. She'd kept his card.

They both stood up, Herschel's chair scraping the floor as he pushed it back. Instantly the kitchen door opened and Sophie was standing there, no doubt she'd been listening on the other side of the door.

"Sophie, please see this gentleman outside," Liz said in a soft tone.

"Yes Ma'am," Sophie almost said, Miss Liz and caught herself. Good thing she'd been listening. *It sounded like Miss Liz was wanted for something by the police.* She also knew it wasn't her place to ask any questions.

Herschel was relieved to be back inside the taxi. Had Reggie been there, he might have been detained. Regardless, Herschel always traveled prepared. Inside the handle of his cane was a sharp stiletto. He hadn't needed to use it for many years, yet it was comforting to have it along, just in case trouble did surface as it sometimes did. It would be useless against someone with a pistol, or someone who came upon him from behind with a garrote.

As soon as he returned to his office, Herschel sent an email message to Nick Alexander informing him of his recent discovery. He'd found Liz working for Reggie Burgoins in his establishment. He also had to agree that Liz looked a lot like Rachel, even with her hair in a different style and color.

Chapter 25

Nick Alexander knew things were beginning to happen when he read Herschel's email message. Liz was alive, even though she was using another name. That meant she was hiding. And now she may attempt to hide again, after being discovered. Her discovery validated Nick's theory that Barry had used her to impersonate Rachel. He wondered if Liz knew where they might find Rachel? If she did, she certainly wouldn't incriminate herself by telling them.

It was time to take a calculated gamble with Barry. As an old fisherman, Nick knew that sometimes you had to use different bait to catch certain types of fish. Not everything worked, so you had to experiment. That's what he decided to do... experiment with a different kind of bait, to hook Barry Greene into revealing where Rachel's body was hidden. He doubted she was alive.

Nick wanted to create a phony front page of the local Smithville newspaper. He stopped by the sheriff's office to ask for their help. A deputy went with Nick over to the newspaper's office, just a few doors away.

The production manager was there. Nick explained what it was he was trying to do. He needed just a front page altered enough to flush out a murder suspect. He further explained that if it didn't work, he'd take full responsibility. That was enough to convince the man to help him.

The dummy front page would be sent to Barry's post office box. Nick got the box number from following him in Ocala earlier. The dummy page from the Smithville newpaper had a big headline:

CORPS OF ENGINEERS TO LOWER CENTER HILL LAKE FOR DAM REPAIRS

The brief article mentioned this would be a one-time opportunity for local authorities to search the lake for stolen vehicles and sunken vessels. Also to do some needed dredging. Nick was gambling on the trunk being hidden there. If so, Barry would be worried about it being found. He'd have to hurry back, locate the abandoned trunk and dispose of it elsewhere, before the water level of Center Hill Lake was lowered. It wouldn't be an easy task. And, there was always the risk that he wouldn't take the bait. Finding the trunk might pose a problem, even for Barry, unless the water was shallow enough and marked by some onshore object to help pinpoint the location.

If Nick's theory was correct, Barry would be heading back to the Smithville area and Center Hill Lake soon.

... Where Nick Alexander, along with the sheriff, would be waiting for Barry's hasty arrival. *Yes, it was just like fishing*, he thought. Once the case was wrapped up, Nick planned to continue his search for something affordable near the lake. That way, Carol wouldn't have far to travel on weekends, or during the week. Or, she could quit working entirely, and help him coordinate some of his mundane background investigations. He was looking forward to wrapping up this mystery, saying farewell to Ezra and getting back to work.

Chapter 26

Ezra Rueben was demanding another update from Nick. Nick decided it was too soon to reveal that Liz had been located. He'd save that item for later. He explained his plan to flush Barry out with the dummy newspaper page he'd mailed.

"I think you should have consulted with me before moving forward so fast. We'll look foolish if he doesn't show up," Ezra said.

Nick thought looking foolish wasn't all that bad considering what the family had been through up to this point. He wished now he'd kept quiet about his plan. Ezra was a man who used people and quickly discarded them after their usefulness. Nick was quickly approaching that limit and knew he had to be careful.

"Have you told the police about your plan?" Ezra asked, still in a huff.

"Yes, the sheriff knows about it. In fact they helped me put together the article. I doubt the newspaper would have gone along with it, if they hadn't agreed to help."

"I have to tell you, Nick, I'm leery about your plan. It could easily backfire."

"Yes it could. So far, nothing else has worked. I've managed to make him uncomfortable, maybe even scare him a little. That only gives us a slight advantage. Now we have to wait and see what he'll do next."

"What if he doesn't react? Then what?"

"I admit it's a gamble. If he doesn't react, then we can safely assume that Rachel's body is hidden elsewhere and eliminate Center Hill Lake from our search."

"I have to alert the McBride agency in Ocala. I want them to keep a close watch on Barry and inform me the minute he leaves for Tennessee."

Since Nick couldn't be in both places at the same time, he had to agree that using the extra resources in Ocala would help. An early alert as to when Barry might arrive would be helpful. They still had to set up a trap and that would take some coordination with the sheriff's department.

That was Nick's next stop, after he got some aspirin and a drink of water to help ease the headache he'd acquired. Ezra had that effect on him. Nick's relationship with all his commercial clients was smooth, never aggravating. His clients appreciated the work he did. In fact, their referrals were the source of most of Nick's new business. So, the tension he felt with Ezra caused him to wonder why he'd bothered to take on this assignment. He actually felt sympathetic toward Barry for his plight, particularly if it turned out that he didn't have anything to do with his wife's disappearance. Nick knew that in the eyes of the law, Barry was presumed innocent until proven otherwise. As a former police officer, it was sometimes difficult to make such an allowance.

As soon as Nick left, Ezra was on the phone to Charles McBride in Ocala. Ezra insisted they maintain a close watch and report back the moment it looked like Barry planned to leave. Ezra also wanted Barry followed, regardless of the destination, so he could receive progress reports en route.

Chapter 27

Charles McBride almost bristled every time Ezra called. Like Nick, he regretted taking the assignment and hoped it would end soon. He'd looked into Ezra's background immediately upon getting the assignment. He wanted to know more about his client. He'd discovered the man was wealthy and could easily afford the bills Charles would be sending. What he didn't discover, until later, was the man was difficult to deal with, even over simple things not worth mentioning. He had to agree with Ezra that Nick's ploy to roust Barry was indeed risky. It would only work if Barry was properly spooked.

So far, Barry's routine was almost predictable; therefore, the agency just did periodic checks, rather than keep the man under continued surveillance, which wasn't warranted. The agency used several different people and rotated them so that Barry wouldn't see the same person too often. Gordon handled the afternoon and evening shift.

From the beginning, they knew Barry was driving a white, late model Ford Explorer, Eddie Bauer edition, with Tennessee plates. Barry hadn't registered the vehicle in Florida yet, making it just a little easier to identify in congested parking lots.

McBride's agency had put an illegal tap on Barry's phone. It proved to be a total waste of time. Barry rarely made a call except to order a pizza, or to alert an elderly lady who did some part-time babysitting for the kid, that he needed her. Sometimes she came to Barry's condo, other times the kid was driven to her house about three miles away.

It seemed that Barry spent time at the library downtown then walked across the square to have a drink and socialize at Harry's. He was never seen leaving with anyone. So, the assignment followed a routine that was almost predictable. There was no indication that Barry was aware of any surveillance until recently. The past week, ever since Ezra's other investigator arrived in Ocala, Gordon reported that Barry had become noticeably nervous, checking other vehicles behind him. As a newcomer to the area, Barry sometimes drove around checking out different neighborhoods. This was understandable since the man sold real estate and was getting some familiarity with his surroundings.

It was fortuitous that Mandy, Charles' nickname for Amanda, happened to meet Barry at Harry's the way she did. If Barry did decide to fly to Belize, they'd know about it instantly, using Mandy's connections. Unfortunately, Barry discovered who Mandy was, and that added to the tension of the moment. It put him on alert that he was being watched. Being cautious, Charles had one of his people attach a transponder to Barry's Explorer soon after getting the surveillance assignment. It was magnetic and fastened directly to the frame underneath and was difficult to detect. The monitor in the office would alert anyone on duty that the Explorer was in motion and where it was, in case Barry wasn't being personally watched.

Charles McBride decided it wasn't necessary to tell Ezra about Barry's recent discovery, of Mandy working for the agency. It was an accident and couldn't have been anticipated. Had Barry attempted to follow her directly to the office, she would have spotted him and diverted to another location like a gas station. She was always careful about things like that.

Now, with the transponder in place, McBride would know if Barry was driving to the airport, which would no doubt be Orlando, of if he was driving north, back to Tennessee.

As soon as they knew what he was up to, provided he took the bait, Charles would call Ezra and alert him of Barry's movement. By following far enough behind, they would know when he stopped for gas, or took an alternate route.

Chapter 28

Liz Miller was now the acknowledged madam at The Lodge. To most of the girls, she was more like a big sister. She made a suggestion to Reggie on how to keep his whores from straying. She suggested that Reggie, or she, open a joint savings account at the local bank for each girl. Money earned could be deposited into their respective accounts every week. The account would be in two names and both signatures would be necessary before any money could be withdrawn.

Once a sizeable amount was accumulated, the woman surely would have to think twice before just taking off. Anyone thinking of leaving would have to ask Reggie for permission and negotiate a release.

Reggie loved the idea. All the working girls at The Lodge thought their status, as well as their future, was more secure, having some money in the bank. Reggie made sure all the girls knew it was Liz's idea. It was really about control. Barry had told Liz earlier, and this just completed the plan nicely. The branch manager at the local bank was one of his occasional clients, so there wouldn't be any suspicious inquiries.

For the first time in ages, Reggie felt completely satisfied. Everything was running smoothly, there were no current problems. Even some of the rougher clients were behaving themselves. With Monique gone, the girls seemed happier, there were fewer arguments and Sophie was always smiling. And, Reggie's personal wealth continued to grow.

The only nagging item was his old buddy, Barry. He wasn't sure if he still trusted Barry. The police might prove his guilt, so Reggie and Liz had to keep their distance. Certainly Reggie wouldn't encourage Barry to make another visit to New Orleans any time soon. If Barry was caught, and convicted of his wife's death, Reggie didn't want to become an accomplice.

Soon after thinking about how well things were going, Liz reported Herschel's surprise visit. She was visibly shaken and couldn't disguise her fear of what might happen next. She and Reggie had discussed Barry's plight at length. She knew she could be considered complicit in his wife's death, making her a fugitive and subject to arrest if the police started to investigate. So far, Monique's disappearance hadn't posed a problem. Reggie doubted that her death would ever be fully investigated, since the police were overloaded. New Orleans had a high crime rate and the chart kept climbing. He knew that from all the newspaper accounts he'd read. Despite the crime, tourists flocked to the Big Easy to become enveloped in its mystique.

Reggie Burgoins had to act fast. He had Herschel's business card that he'd left, and knew exactly where the man's office was located in the Garden District. *One surprise visit deserved another*, he thought. He didn't have time to check out the man, before taking a taxi into the popular area. Every time he visited the Garden District, he was reminded of the sharp contrast with his own seedy neighborhood. The Garden District had always been a showcase, and major attraction, for visitors. All the big homes were nicely maintained and well-landscaped. It was evidence of a graceful era. Even the air smelled better, he thought.

He dressed for the visit so he wouldn't look out of place. The taxi parked down the block, after circling twice, to give Reggie some idea of any and all possible escape routes. The taxi driver was instructed to wait for him. Since it was Reggie, his reputation was enough, to make sure the taxi driver didn't take off on him, or accept another fare. Reggie could tell the taxi driver was nervous, expecting something bad to happen. The black man's face and forehead was covered with sweat.

"How long you goin' to be, boss?"

"I don't know. Not too long. It doesn't matter though. You'd better be here when I come out, hear me?"

The office occupied the bottom floor of a three-story, century-old mansion with a wrap-around porch, complete with white rocking chairs and hanging plants. The front door to Herschel's office was unlocked. A small brass plate had Herschel's name engraved. It was the only hint that this was his office. Reggie was surprised to see a receptionist sitting in the reception area, working at her desk.

"Can I help you?" the young lady asked.

"I'd like to inquire about the services you provide here," Reggie lied.

"Certainly. May I ask how you learned about us? Did someone refer us?"

"Yes, I think it was a taxi driver who mentioned something about you people doing private investigations."

"That was probably Dooley. He sends us a lot of customers. What exactly do you need to have investigated Mr. ahhh...?"

"My name is Raymond. Raymond Collins. I guess I'd prefer to discuss my problem with one of your investigators. Is someone available?"

"Of course. Just have a seat, Mister Collins and I'll be right back." With that the woman left the room, leaving a fragrant trail. She didn't use the phone, or intercom.

A few moments later, she re-appeared and ushered him into Herschel's office off a hallway in the rear of the building. As soon as she made the introductions, she left closing the door behind her, for added privacy. Reggie was impressed with her professionalism, as well as the all the office furnishings. There was a fern stand in a bay window overlooking a parking lot at the rear of the building. The parking lot, Reggie noted, was accessed by an alley. At one time there had been a garage. Now it was a parking lot.

"Please have a seat Mr. Collins." Herschel didn't rise or make any attempt to shake hands. "Now, what is it I can do for you?"

"I'd like to have you find someone for me."

"Is this something that would be better handled by the police?"

"No, I don't want the police involved."

"I see. Do you have a picture of this person?"

"Yes, she's my aunt and she's been missing for a few weeks now." Reggie took out a photo he'd taken of Monique a year earlier. She looked a lot like Tina Turner, the singer.

"I must say, she's a striking woman. Does she live here in New Orleans?"

"Yes, she does. She used to call me every week. She was an entertainer although I can't tell you exactly where she worked, she never said."

"Hmm. Do you have a home address for her?"

"Yes, but she's not there. She lives in an apartment house with her boyfriend who seems to have vanished as well. He was a few years younger than her." Reggie was trying to anticipate questions, so he'd have a ready response.

"I see. Do you suppose they left together? Perhaps they took a trip, or a short vacation."

"I don't think so. She would have told me. How much do you charge to do an investigation like this?" Reggie was sizing up the office, looking for a rear entrance. His plan was to get the big man out of the office.

Herschel's instincts told him the man was here under false pretenses. He saw his eyes taking in all the surroundings, just like a thief might do when casing a place he planned to rob later. And, there was a slight hesitation before answering, along with a blinking that told Herschel the man was lying. This was a ruse and he had to be careful. He pushed a button on the inside of his desk with his knee. It was a silenced buzzer that only his secretary could hear. Whenever it buzzed, she'd been instructed to summon Dooley. Usually it meant he was getting ready to leave.

"My fee is four hundred dollars a day... plus expenses. I require a two-day advance when I start an assignment."

"That's reasonable enough. Can I pay you now and call you later with some additional details? I didn't bring everything with me today."

"Certainly. Bring anything you think would be helpful. I'd like the name of her boyfriend and where either of them worked. That's where I'll start."

"Will you be doing the investigating, or will it be someone else?"

"I'll probably handle it personally, unless you have some objection."

"Oh no, that's fine. I was hoping you'd do it, rather than someone else, less experienced."

"How very kind of you." Herschel rose and extended his hand to accept the money and shake the man's hand. He noticed the manicure. "If it isn't too inconvenient, Mr. Collins, please give my assistant your address and phone number so I know how to contact you. And I'll look forward to the rest of the information you'll be getting for me. Good day to you, sir."

As Reggie rose and handed the money over to the big man, the office door opened on cue. Reggie gave the woman a false address and phone number. When he left, he walked down the block to the waiting taxi. Without looking over his shoulder, he had a feeling his departure was being observed.

Reggie had some idea of the first floor layout. He noticed the back door opened into a hallway. With the parking area behind the house, it was possible to drive through the alleyway and pull in behind the building. It wasn't entirely secluded, but it would do.

It was too chancy to have the taxi drive up the alleyway. Instead, Reggie got out again at the end of the block and walked part way up the alley. There was just one car parked behind the house, an older model Ford Escort with a faded roof. Reggie hoped it belonged to the receptionist. He couldn't imagine the fat guy getting into anything that small.

Reggie had to wait until the receptionist left. Then, he could go back carrying a large envelope, pretending he had some items to drop off. Hopefully the front door would be locked and he could knock at the back door, holding up the envelope. It would be enough for the fat guy to open the door, after recognizing him.

And that would be the fat man's last mistake.

Chapter 29

Barry Greene read the newspaper clipping several times. The article mentioned the water level of the lake would be lowered, beginning this coming Friday. That only gave him three days to get back to Smithville undetected. He was pretty sure he was still being watched. He wondered who sent the clipping. The envelope had a Smithville postmark. And he hadn't given anyone there his post office box number, so it had to be Ezra playing some sort of trick on him.

Or, maybe it was that smart-ass investigator that suddenly showed up asking questions. He could have followed Barry to the post office and learned his box number. That same investigator had also learned about Liz. The guy bothered him. He acted too confident, like he knew more than he was letting on, slipping it out in pieces.

Liz was no longer in the picture, unless Reggie screwed it up. He wished he could contact Reggie, but the email message said he was going to be unavailable. Reggie never seemed to be worried about anything, yet his note sounded like he was more than a little concerned.

Barry knew that Reggie was used to being hounded by the police and never expressed any real concern. His girls serviced several of the local police and politicians, keeping him reasonably protected. For Reggie it was just part of doing business. He even kept some illegal and very expensive Cuban cigars on hand for a few preferred clients. So why was he so suddenly worried? Did it have something to do with Liz?

Barry had given Liz, Reggie's phone number with instructions to call him as soon as she arrived in New Orleans. Reggie already knew she was coming, had her flight number and time of arrival. So even if she didn't call, Reggie would have made contact. He had a description of her, but Barry suspected she surprised Reggie by being considerably more attractive than he expected. Barry guessed the red hair would captivate Reggie the moment he met her. Barry and Reggie had that in common; both were attracted to red heads.

Knowing his friend, Reggie probably had some fun with Liz for a night or two before terminating her. Barry wished there had been some other option. Alive, Liz posed a threat to him, once she discovered Rachel was missing and that she'd been an accomplice after the fact. That bit of knowledge could translate into big bucks. She could force Barry to pay to keep it a secret, or she could sell what she knew to Ezra. Either way it spelled a financial nightmare. Thanks to Reggie, it was too late now to worry about. Still, he missed her and reflected back on the many good times they'd had together. She'd even come through for him when he needed her help. Of course she also did it for the money, like the whore she always was.

Two days after Liz arrived in New Orleans, Reggie called collect to report everything had been taken care of, just as Barry had asked. Much later, Reggie had sent an email message hinting that Barry *owed him big time*. That could only mean one thing, that Reggie had wasted Liz, just as he'd instructed, and like the vile person he was, felt the need to remind Barry of the favor rendered.

Now Reggie was the only real impediment if the police started asking new questions. Barry had to get back to Smithville fast, to take care of one other detail he couldn't afford to have discovered.

Chapter 30

Barry Greene had to consider his next move. The damned lake was about to reveal a secret that would cause him additional problems.

Before going to the office that Monday, *after Rachel left him stranded,* Barry had stopped back to the boat launch area where he'd met Liz. The new lock was in place and he had the key. Liz's Honda Civic was still there, hidden from view by a stand of Pines so anyone passing by on the main highway wouldn't see it. He couldn't afford to have it spotted by a passing police cruiser who would surely want to investigate why it was there.

Barry had her car keys. It took several tries before the engine started. It needed a tune-up badly. Barry drove the car to the broken ascending concrete slab that disappeared into the water. At one time this ramp was used to put smaller boats, on trailers, into the water. Years of decay had taken its toll, it was badly cracked. He left the car in drive and jumped out, watching the car move slowly forward and downward, eventually disappearing below the surface of the water. He'd removed the license plate earlier and discarded it on the way to the office. He also remembered to lock the gate once he left, throwing away the key. With the gate locked, it was doubtful anyone would attempt to use the closed ramp and discover the car.

Now he wished he'd kept that key. He had to get back, find someone who could remove the sunken auto and dispose of it, before the water level dropped, exposing the one remaining link he had to Liz. Liz was supposed to call and report her car stolen, on her way to the airport, or from the airport lobby. He wasn't sure if she had remembered to do it. She was nervous when she left that Sunday morning and probably forgot. Thinking back, reporting it stolen wasn't a good idea, either. What was Liz supposed to drive upon her return? Shit, things had happened too fast that day. He thought he had all the bases covered, but now that he looked back on the events, there were a few holes.

If the police found Liz's old Honda Civic in the lake, and if that investigator told the police about his involvement with Liz, a whole new line of questions would surely follow. Once Barry's involvement with Liz was established, it would be enough for Ezra to win a custody suit over Jonathan and point additional suspicion at him, even though he knew they'd never find Rachel's body. Never the less, circumstantial evidence had a way of convincing juries. Ezra could paint a convincing picture.

It was crucial that Liz's Honda wasn't discovered.

Barry estimated it would take at least ten hours to drive to Smithville, stopping only for gas along the way, provided there wasn't traffic problems, construction or accidents. Interstate 75 had heavy traffic all hours of the day and night.

Before he left, he had some arrangements to make with the babysitter. He didn't want to take Jonathan along. Being that close to his grandparents, he'd want to visit them and Jake, his dog. The boy missed the dog, missed his mother and was becoming difficult every time Barry had to leave him.

Barry packed a small overnight bag, put it inside a plastic trash bag, to disguise it, and walked out to his

Explorer. Anyone watching would think he was taking out some trash. He packed another bag for Jonathan and did the same thing. He tried to explain to his son that he'd be back soon. Fortunately the boy liked Mrs. Pearlman, the old lady who watched him. And he loved playing with her dog.

"Are you going to look for mommy?" Jonathan asked.

"Boy, you are so smart. Yes, that's exactly what I'm going to do." Later Barry would consider just how insightful the question was.

While driving to the babysitter's house, Barry was conscious of a black Jeep Cherokee staying several vehicles behind him. He was fairly certain he was being followed. He couldn't panic, he had to remain calm, act like this was another routine trip.

The babysitter was pleased to see Jonathan and he seemed happy to see her. The dog was always happy when Jonathan showed up. Seeing this, Barry made a mental note that one day, when they were finally settled somewhere, he'd buy his son another dog.

Barry used Mrs. Pearlman's telephone to call a local service garage he'd used for some minor repairs and oil changes. He said he wanted to leave his Explorer for a few days, to have it serviced while he was gone. Next he called a local car rental agency and asked if they had any SUVs available? They did, and he requested they pick him up at the service shop. With those arrangements made, he said goodbye to Jonathan promising to call him later.

As he was driving away, Barry had a sudden weird thought. What if this was just a ruse, to get him to leave Jonathan, so Ezra could snatch him and take him back to Smithville? Barry looked in the rearview mirror for the Jeep Cherokee and didn't see it. If he'd seen the Jeep, he would have turned around, picked up his son and taken Jonathan with him. Paranoia was beginning to re-establish itself and Barry didn't like the way it clouded his thinking. He'd always been good at solving problems, but he could only do it with clear concentration and nothing fuzzy lingering along the sidelines.

His last impulsive decision had been costly. One more like that and he wouldn't be making any more decisions, they'd be made for him ... behind bars somewhere. He couldn't afford to let that happen.

He could still see it, they'd had one of their usual arguments. Barry walked out of the house and into the back yard, ignoring her. She'd followed him, not finished with her berating, reminding him, "if it wasn't for my family, you'd still be living in a one-bedroom apartment, selling cars six days a week". He'd just learned that Ezra had suggested the family take a cruise together. It would be just Ezra, Maureen, Rachel and Jonathan. Barry had learned about it by accident. Apparently he wasn't invited. Later, Ezra explained that he thought it would be better if Barry stayed, to manage things in the Smithville office, even though things were slow. It was just another of Ezra's many slights. It wasn't even subtle.

Perhaps ten days alone would be a different kind of vacation, he thought then. Still, it was the ultimate slap in the face, even though Rachel didn't see it that way. When Rachel turned her back to him, in anger, Barry picked up a large rock, sitting beside the patio, and hit her over the head. She crumpled to the ground without a sound. There wasn't any blood, to his surprise.

It was over just like that, and he had to suddenly shift gears and consider what he'd just done, and what to do next. At the time, he didn't really have a well thought out plan. It just happened. Because it happened in the back yard, no one saw, or heard anything. Thankfully, Jonathan was with his grandmother, Maureen.

While driving, Barry thought back to that fateful hot Friday afternoon. Removing the trunk from the houseboat had been easy enough. Barry had to wait until Odell left on an errand, so he wouldn't see Barry's Explorer. He'd found an old abandoned rock quarry that hadn't been used in years. The quarry was on the same road that led down to the marina. There was a sharp curve in the road and a grassy level spot just large enough to park. His Explorer could be seen from the road, but being on the sharp curve, and partially hidden by brush, it would be just a brief sighting at best. It was a chance he had to take, hoping not to be seen.

The road was called Floating Mill Road and the quarry was overgrown with brush and trees bordered it. If a person didn't know about the quarry being there, they'd surely miss it. Barry dragged the trunk down a steep rocky slope using a plastic tarp as a skid. He used three bags of lime, pouring them over Rachel's folded corpse. Using a pair of leather work gloves, it had taken a half hour to gather and pile enough rocks and dirt over the trunk to keep it from ever being discovered. He took the empty limestone bags him and disposed of them at a dumpsite on Highway 56 north of the road that led to the marina. He was exhausted by the time he was finished.

It wouldn't take too long for Rachel's body to decompose, he thought. The lime and rocks would kill any smell, so discovery was almost impossible.

On the way home he pulled up to a pay phone and called Liz at work hoping he'd reach her. He didn't want to use his cell phone and have the call recorded somewhere. As soon as he returned home he took a shower. He didn't have much time before he'd be meeting Liz at the abandoned boat launch area. He had to stop by the Ace Hardware to buy a pair of bolt cutters and a new lock.

Searching for Rachel

Now, he alone knew where Rachel's body was hidden. He didn't plan to share that information with anyone, ever. Without her body, the police might suspect him, but they'd never be able to prove he'd killed her. It wasn't something he'd planned. It wasn't premeditated. In a crazy kind of way, he could almost rationalize it as self defense. If someone had ever asked what the motive was, he'd have had to say it was because he hated his father-in-law and all his manipulation. His anger had actually been misplaced. Ezra should have been his intended target, now that he thought about it. Too late.

Driving to the marina with Liz later, in Rachel's convertible, was easy enough. He left the top up. Anyone who saw the car would immediately think Rachel was there. He called Liz by Rachel's name while Odell helped him untie the houseboat.

Barry was still re-living that day as he drove north on Interstate 75, trying to stay just above the speed limit. While concentrating on the road, he was trying to think whom he might get to drag Liz's Honda out of the water. He'd stopped by the bank earlier and now had a thousand dollars on him. For what he wanted done, nobody would take a check, it would be cash only and quickly forgotten. He'd have to make up some sort of story about why and how the car was there in the water.

Killing Rachel wasn't something he'd ever be able to forget. He'd put it away in the back of his mind, hoping other events would replace his thoughts. Then as he'd drift off to sleep, he'd see Rachel turning around and looking at him with a furious frown on her face asking why? The nightmare persisted. Barry hoped that over time it would evaporate. It didn't. He was haunted by that same bad dream at least once a week.

No one would ever understand the torment he'd caused to himself by such a rash and stupid act of violence. It was too late to say it was an accident. It was something he'd just have to live with, just like Reggie would have to live with disposing of Liz. Reggie probably didn't have those same type nightmares, however. For him, killing was a way of life. That was a scary thought.

Searching for Rachel

Chapter 31

Charles McBride was irate when his associate called to say that they'd lost Barry. They thought he'd taken his Explorer in for service. They never saw him leave in another vehicle, so they'd waited several hours before discovering he was gone. The mechanic told them Barry wasn't expected back until Monday.

Charles McBride didn't want to lose Ezra as a client under circumstances like this. He hated to make the next call.

"I believe your son-in-law is on his way back to Smithville," Charles reported.

"What do you mean, *you believe*. Is he, or isn't he?"

"He left about three hours ago, by our calculation. He must have spotted my man who was tailing him. Either that, or he was just lucky. He dropped off his kid with the babysitter, left his Explorer at a service garage and apparently rented another SUV for the weekend. That's as much as we know."

"What type and color vehicle did he rent?"

"It's a black Ford Expedition. It will have Florida plates. I can get the license plate number for you."

"I should have thought you'd already done that. Call me back when you have that information ... and don't make me wait."

Ezra Rueben doubted that Barry would return to his former house. In any event, Ezra already had the locks changed. Since Barry wasn't being followed, there were several routes he could take once he got to Chattanooga. Ezra tried to envision the most direct way, coming up Route 111 to Sparta, then taking Highway 70 west into Smithville. That would be the way he'd do it.

As an added precaution, he called the marina, where the houseboat was docked, and asked that anyone seeing Barry should notify him at once. He also needed to station someone along Highway 70 to be on the lookout for the black SUV when it arrived, then follow it at a discreet distance. Perhaps he could hire one of the off-duty deputies.

Deputy Randy Cooper took Ezra's call. He was also the officer who spoke with the private investigator who'd stopped by last week. He listened and took notes. Finally he decided he could use the extra money and agreed to park alongside the highway and wait for the designated black SUV to pass by. He could do it while still on-duty and make out.

Calculating the elapsed time since Barry left, and that time was a bit uncertain, he needed to be in place an hour before his shift ended. Hopefully there wouldn't be any urgent calls requiring him to be someplace else.

Randy anticipated waiting a few hours. He had time to grab a quick sandwich at McDonald's, refill his thermos with hot coffee and find a suitable place to wait. Ezra said he'd pay $500 for the quick surveillance. Deputy Cooper assumed he would pay in cash. It would be enough for a down payment on a used motorcycle he had his eye on. As much as he disliked old man Rueben, he didn't mind taking some of his money. It was even better when it was tax free.

Searching for Rachel

Randy knew the perfect spot, about a mile inside the county line. The highway snaked down to the river forcing drivers to slow down, because of all the curves, before crossing the Sligo Bridge. The Sligo Marina was on one side of the rather narrow bridge. Then the two-lane highway snaked upwards again with several more tricky curves. Deputy Cooper, still in a patrol car, parked, by backing in at an angle to the highway. He was hidden from anyone coming down the hill from Sparta. From this same spot, he'd snagged many speeding motorists coming down that hill. Randy took frequent sips from the thermos to help occupy him while he waited.

While waiting, several vehicles sped by, well over the speed limit. He couldn't risk going after them for fear of missing Barry.

Using his cell phone, Randy called Ezra just to let him know he was in position and waiting. Ezra gave him the license plate number of the black Ford Expedition he was looking for so he wouldn't accidentally follow the wrong vehicle. Ezra asked if Deputy Cooper was still in uniform and driving his patrol car? He was hoping he would be.

Two extremely long hours passed before the black SUV appeared, speeding down the hill. Deputy Cooper watched as it crossed the bridge before pulling out to follow. He called Ezra to report spotting Barry and to say he was following at a discrete distance.

Chapter 32

Herschel Fielding had an uneasy feeling after his new client left. Something was wrong about the entire exchange. He felt sure the man was there under false pretenses.

Sarah, his assistant had called Dooley. It was a little earlier than normal to pick up Herschel. As always, Dooley came around to the back, rather than wait in front. Herschel didn't like to make his departures known to anyone curious about his activity. It was an old habit that went back to his prosecutor days. Herschel kept a pistol in his right hand desk drawer, within easy reach. He seldom carried it with him. This evening he made an exception, putting the piece into his pocket. In his business, one survived because of good instincts. More than once he had to remind himself of that.

Dooley pulled into the alleyway and saw a man approaching Herschel's back door. As he drew nearer, he recognized the man and honked his horn leaning out the window.

"Hey Reggie, how's it going?" Dooley called.

At that precise moment Herschel looked out the window of his office and saw his new client approaching the rear of the building, carrying a large manila envelope. Then he heard Dooley call to the man, calling him Reggie!

Herschel had never met the man, known as Reggie, before and only knew him by his colorful reputation.

With that, everything fell into place. Herschel knew instantly that Dooley probably saved his life, by calling out the man's name. Dooley had no awareness of what happened earlier. It was all just a matter of chance as so often happens in life.

Herschel waved to Dooley, turned and locked the back door putting the keys into the same pocket as the pistol. He walked toward Reggie keeping his hand in his pocket.

"That was pretty fast," Herschel said, nodding toward the envelope.

"Yes, but I forgot a few items. I'll stop back tomorrow with everything," Reggie said. The man was attempting to leave in a hurry.

"Fine. And may I suggest that you utilize the front entrance next time. Only thieves and hired help use the back entrance. I trust you don't fit into either of those categories, Mr. Burgoins."

"So you know who I am?" Reggie stopped and turned around.

"Yes, and I also know why you're here. Your friend Liz Miller must have mentioned my earlier visit to your establishment. I suspect you feel threatened, as you should."

"Okay, so what do you plan to do about it?"

"Do? I've already done what I set out to do. I found the missing woman known as Liz Miller and reported it to my client. That's the extent of my involvement. What I plan to do now, is enjoy a good cigar and meal at one of my favorite eating establishments." As an after thought he added, "Feel free to join me and we can discuss your unusual predicament." He still had the man's money and didn't intend to return it under the circumstances, bizarre as they were.

Reggie considered his situation. He was caught trying to bluff the big man, who wasn't the least concerned about his welfare. His driver was still there waiting, and he'd just been invited to dine with the man he'd come to kill. It was a crazy situation, unlike any he'd been confronted with. They were both buying time.

"Okay," Reggie said. He'd play along and hope to learn something. He dismissed his waiting taxi, after paying the fare, and got into Dooley's cab, sitting in the front seat.

"It's good of you to join me. I trust you aren't armed. If you are, kindly present your weapon to Dooley. He'll keep it and return it when we're finished and has driven you back to your establishment. Clever name for a bordello."

"Thank you. Not everyone gets it." Reggie passed over his knife and Dooley accepted it while continuing to drive.

"What would you have done if your taxi hadn't shown up when he did?" Reggie asked, testing the wine in his glass.

"I would have waited for you to make your move, then I would have shot you, making sure you were dead before calling one of my friends in the police department."

"So your client already knows about Liz. Is there any way I can protect her?" He wanted to add, and keep her from testifying against Barry, but there was no reason to expand his predicament more than it already was. "I don't want to lose her."

"And you were willing to kill me just to keep her secret?"

"I know that sounds crazy to you, but yes, I would do anything for her. She's the first woman I have truly loved." It was a confession he hadn't plan to make. He hadn't said as much to Liz yet, although he intended to.

Searching for Rachel

"You are trying to appeal to my romantic inclinations, sir." Herschel paused while he collected his thoughts and drew on his cigar, exhaling the smoke upward. "Here's what I want from you and Liz. I want you both to sign statements about what you know about Rachel Greene's sudden disappearance and what your involvement was with Barry. I'll have Dooley pick them up tomorrow. Then I suggest the two of you take an immediate vacation to some remote place where they've never heard of either of you. Consider yourselves in exile for a while. Call me from time to time and I'll tell you when it's safe to return."

"Why are you doing this?"

"Because you didn't kill Liz, like everyone thought. And because, it appears you have fallen in love with a lovely lady, who was probably duped, by that cad Barry Greene. Also, I have eight hundred dollars of your money, minus the cost of dinner tonight. You are, after all, one of my clients." Conflict of interest never bothered Herschel.

"You are an extraordinary man, Mr. Fielding. I'm glad now that I didn't kill you," Reggie laughed. He didn't doubt the man's integrity.

"Me too," Herschel said followed by a deep chuckle. He offered Reggie a premium cigar. "Who knows, I may even become one of your clients one day." It was a frivolous thought, but he was in a frivolous mood, having survived a precarious afternoon that could have ended badly. Instead, he'd be able to send Nick some additional information confirming what they'd already suspected.

He planned to give his friend, Dooley a nice surprise bonus for his prompt arrival.

Dooley was waiting, acting impatient, which was quite unlike him. "We must hurry, boss. I just heard on the radio, there's a terrible storm approaching. They're calling it Hurricane Katrina and they're talking about evacuation plans in case it hits here."

Chapter 33

Barry Greene was making good time. The weather conditions were favorable and the traffic had been light, once he was past Chattanooga. He'd kept an eye open for any vehicle that remained behind him for a prolonged period. Once, just before reaching Atlanta, he pulled into a rest stop and immediately left again checking to see if a familiar vehicle did the same maneuver.

He felt fairly certain now that he wasn't being followed. The Ford Excursion was a bigger vehicle than his Explorer. It rode better and seemed to handle differently. Barry kept it on cruise control as much as possible having it set just five mph over the speed limit, that way he could remain with most of the traffic and not draw any undo attention. He certainly didn't need to get stopped for speeding.

Traffic was light on Route 111 and he made good time, still remaining just over the speed limit, except when he was passing through Spencer, where he slowed down. Sure enough a state highway patrol car was sitting at a gas station as he passed by, remaining at the lowered speed limit. He kept his eyes on the rearview mirror half expecting to be followed. He took a deep breath and was relieved when the patrol car didn't move.

Searching for Rachel

Once he was on Highway 70, going west out of Sparta, he knew the two-lane road well, waiting to pass several vehicles poking along at the speed limit. Now he was eager to get everything finished. He was almost there and suddenly felt tired. He'd been running on adrenalin for the past ten hours and now his body was reacting to a lack of sleep.

Barry's impatience was growing by the time he crossed the line into DeKalb County. He knew all the curves and was able to negotiate them all the while maintaining a speed just over sixty. He was aware that this larger SUV didn't handle the curves as well as his Explorer due to a different center of gravity. Just before crossing the river, he spotted a sheriff's patrol car sitting back on the left side of the road, at the bottom of the long winding road. In the past, he'd been aware of this popular radar trap.

He watched in his rearview mirror and saw the patrol car pull out and begin to follow him. No flashing light bar, just remaining behind him at a steady pace.

Ezra Rueben received the call from the off-duty Deputy, Randy Cooper that he was following a black Ford Expedition with Florida plates. They were on highway 70, driving west toward Smithville. "Just a male driver inside the vehicle," he reported. "We can't be sure it's your son-in-law driving the vehicle, unless I stop him and check his identification. I did clock him at five miles an hour over the speed limit, coming down that hill."

"Go ahead, stop him! We might as well document that he's back in the area, even if it's just for a short period. Ask him where he's going while you're at it," Ezra yelled.

"Yes sir. I'll keep you posted."

Chapter 34

Barry Greene remained at the speed limit, all the while negotiating several uphill curves. Suddenly the light bar started flashing behind him.

For a brief moment, Barry was tempted to stomp on the accelerator and outrun the patrol car, but it would be a foolish, impulsive thing to do. A roadblock could be set up in a matter of a few minutes and he'd have to explain himself. The less attention paid to his presence, the better. He pulled over, lowered the window and reached for the rental agreement in the glove compartment.

Suddenly he felt tired. He hadn't slept in over 24 hours and was surviving on caffeine that was making him jittery.

"So Mr. Greene, what brings you back to our part of the country?" The deputy noted that Barry still used a Tennessee driver's license, even though he was known to be living in Florida.

"I plan to spend the weekend with some old friends I haven't seen for a while. Is there a problem officer?"

"As a matter of fact there is. You were going five over the limit, when you came down that hill before crossing the bridge. I'm going to give you a citation for speeding. And since you're now living in another state, I'll need a local address where you'll be staying while you're visiting. You can mail in the fine."

"No favors for people who live here?"

"No sir. Even though you still have a local address on your driver's license, we know for a fact that you're living in Florida, so you're not considered a local resident anymore. Even if you were, and I gave you a break, I'd be in a lot of trouble. I suggest you get a Florida license one of these days, this one will be expiring soon." Randy was being as polite as possible.

Ever since that private investigator showed up on his doorstep, nothing seemed to be going right, Barry thought. Now this ridiculous ticket. Barry didn't like the fact that there was any kind of documentation to prove his reappearance in Smithville. If Ezra knew he was back, there would surely be a confrontation. After driving ten hours and not having anything to eat, he just didn't want to think about details.

He needed a few hours of sleep, find someone to get rid of Liz's Honda and get back home as fast as possible. With all the confusion going on, he'd forgotten to check his passport as he'd intended to do. With any luck, it was still valid. He needed a week's vacation in Belize. He could almost feel the warm ocean breeze as he laid on the beach watching bikini-clad young things wiggle by. That's what he needed. He'd make reservations as soon as he got back. It would be a reward for making this hectic trip.

Suddenly he was being asked to sign the citation and he was back to the present.

"By the way, when are they lowering the lake for the dam repairs?" Barry asked.

"Don't know anything about it. This is the first I've heard." Deputy Cooper wasn't in the office when Nick came in to get some help with the newspaper dummy, so he hadn't heard about the ruse. It hadn't been openly discussed and he hadn't seen the sheriff at all that day.

It was a trap! He'd felt it, but was still uncertain, until this very moment. They'd been waiting for his arrival, planning to follow him, catch him trying to retrieve Liz's Honda. It had to be a trap, other wise a local police officer would certainly know if the water level of the lake was being lowered. It would be a popular topic and everyone around this lake community would be talking about it. Now there was no need now for him to stick around, or worry about Liz's abandoned car. It was time to say adios and get out of Dodge. He'd driven all this way for nothing.

Barry signed the ticket, re-fastened his seat belt, started the engine and waited for the deputy to pull out. However, the deputy seemed to remain stationed behind him for several minutes, each waiting for the other to pull out

Getting impatient, Barry's annoyance kicked into overdrive. He wasn't about to fall into any trap Ezra had waiting for him. Tired of waiting, he pulled out onto the highway without signaling, did a fast u-turn and headed back the way he came. This time, he totally disregarded the speed limit.

Barry was getting out of the area fast, before they played any more cute tricks. He'd pick up his son and find someplace else to live. Maybe go to Belize permanently and not tell anyone where he was. Mexico was even closer.

Barry's surprise departure left the deputy in a momentary quandary. He speed-dialed Ezra and reported what happened, all the while making a similar u-turn onto the highway. Even with his light bar flashing, he had to wait for traffic before pulling out on the busy highway.

"Don't let him get away!" Ezra shouted over the phone. That dumb-ass trick the private investigator thought up had backfired after all. He couldn't rely on anyone to do what needed to be done. It had always been that way. You delegated then checked to see that what you had delegated was in fact being done properly. Usually someone screwed it up, or overlooked something, just like now, he thought.

Barry saw the patrol car pull out, turn around and with the light bar flashing and the siren going, it started to gain on him. This time, Barry stomped on the accelerator and watched as his speed began to climb past 80. He flew past the bridge and didn't slow down for the upcoming curves ahead. The patrol car was still in pursuit, but no longer gaining on him.

Barry checked the speedometer. He was up to 90, with the needle still moving.

He felt the big SUV lean as he negotiated the first curve. Then the road curved in the opposite direction, causing the vehicle to sway and skid. Barry tried not to overcorrect and stayed off the brakes. He knew the center of gravity was higher on this vehicle than his Explorer, neither of which handled like a sports car on curves at high speed.

Barry accelerated to prevent the skid, crossing the double yellow centerline. He checked his speed again, then the rearview mirror. When he looked up, Barry knew in that very instant, that it was too late to avoid hitting the oncoming gravel truck that was blasting its horn.

"Nooooooooo!" He heard himself yelling above the roar of the engine.

The head on collision was heard a mile away. The impact collapsed the front end of the SUV, forcing the engine into the front seat, taking parts of Barry, and the air bags, with it. Smoke turned into flames a minute later followed by a huge explosion and resulting fire ball.

Chapter 35

Ezra Rueben was among the first to learn of the accident. The deputy following Barry arrived seconds later and called 911 instantly, before getting out his cruiser to vomit. It was by far the worst accident he'd ever witnessed. The driver of the gravel truck was severely injured, requiring an air ambulance to Nashville. So far, Barry was the only fatality, but it didn't look promising for the other driver. Flares were set up on Highway 70 to alert oncoming vehicles in both directions. There wasn't room for any traffic to drive around the burning remains. Even the black topped highway was melting from the intense heat.

"All I wanted, was for you to follow him," Ezra ranted when he got the news from the deputy. Barry was his only hope of ever finding Rachel's body, which was probably in the lake somewhere, stuffed into that damned trunk Maureen insisted on buying.

"No sir, you said to 'stop him, which I did. I even wrote a ticket, so we know it was him, not somebody else driving that SUV. For some reason, and I'm damned if I know what it was, he suddenly got spooked. When he pulled out, he did a uturn and punched it. I had trouble trying to keep up with him. He was flying." It annoyed Randy that Ezra didn't remember his earlier exact orders.

"He was doing over ninety going up that hill when he lost it," Randy added.

"I don't recall giving you such an order," Ezra screamed, then hung up. His next call was to Charles McBride in Ocala.

"I want you to pick up my grandson. You know where he's staying. I'll charter a jet and meet you at the Ocala airport in a few hours. Just wait for me there."

"What about Barry?" Charles asked. "Did he ever show up?"

"He's dead. Killed in a bad crash here, with a big truck." Ezra had no remorse. *In fact, custody would no longer be an issue*, he thought..

"I'm going with you," Maureen insisted. She hated to fly in small aircraft, even though it was a chartered jet. She was making an exception. "And, we're taking Jake along with us."

Taking Jake would help distract Jonathan from all the pain. She tried to think how she'd be able to explain to the boy that both his parents were dead. She felt sad and yet relieved that Barry was no longer a thorn. Perhaps now Ezra would relax more, and start enjoying the fruits of all his enterprise. That was her hope, but something down deep inside told her not to bet on it.

On his way to the airport, Ezra called his Smithville office. "I want a for sale sign put up immediately," he instructed one of the sales agents on duty. "Make sure it states, by appointment only," He wanted the sign to be prominently displayed on the front lawn of Barry and Rachel's house. *No need for it to remain vacant any longer*, he thought.

Chapter 36

Nick Alexander heard about Barry's accident and most of the related details from the sheriff. The trap almost worked. He decided not to send Ezra a bill for his services, just the expenses, including the trips to New Orleans and Ocala. He wouldn't include any of the fees paid to Herschel Fielding, he'd absorb those, grateful for the opportunity to know the man and become his friend.

Keeping his bill simple would avoid some nasty comments and haggling with Ezra over the results of the investigation. Nick wasn't in the mood to listen to anything Ezra had to say at this point. *The man could rationalize just about anything.*

Rachel Greene's remains would continue to be an unsolved mystery. Had Barry not been stopped, Nick was convinced they might have found her body, or at least gathered some additional useful information that would have led to an eventual discovery.

Nick wasn't happy the way the assignment ended, but knew that Barry's actions were beyond his control, even though he played a part in baiting him to return to Smithville.

Ezra's intervention prevented the investigation from moving forward. Nick could sympathize with the sheriff and his staff for all they had to endure, during their earlier search. The sheriff indicated that he wasn't too happy about his deputy taking orders, from a civilian, while he was supposedly still on-duty. Ezra didn't run his department and the sheriff had already decided he didn't need the man's financial support if he decided to run again.

Herschel had faxed Reggie's and Liz's statements. It was the last thing Herschel would do before evacuating with Dooley to Mobile, hoping to avoid the storm. He'd learned that Reggie and Liz had already left for parts unknown. Herschel doubted he would ever hear from either of them again. The statements he sent helped confirm what Nick suspected, that Barry was responsible for Rachel's disappearance and probable death. Barry's motive was still unclear, and would remain a mystery.

Nick dropped off all his notes, photos and documents with the sheriff, just in case the investigation should continue later. As a cold case it was unlikely. It was doubtful Ezra would continue to pursue it.

"In a weird sort of way, Barry did all of us a favor, didn't he?" Sheriff Bobby Joe said.

"Yeah. I think it really bugged Ezra that Barry was fooling around behind Rachel's back and he hadn't learned about it earlier," Nick said waving to the sheriff as he left.

"Stop back, any time hear," the sheriff called after him. *For a Yankee he wasn't a half-bad guy. He'd kept his promise, keeping me in the loop.*

It wouldn't be anytime soon, Nick decided. He had to re-think his plans about living on, or near the lake. Living in a small town, like Cookeville, was looking more appealing all the time. Perhaps he and Carol would just invest in some remodeling of her house. Nick thought adding a post lamp beside the front walk might be a nice addition. And perhaps a sign hanging from the cross bar, telling everyone who passed by, the Alexanders lived there.

"I think Barry was trapped by his greed and Ezra Rueben's money," Carol said, after hearing Nick's recap. "It's too bad it had to end that way."

"Hmm. I think it ended just the way Ezra wanted it to end, with Barry permanently out of the picture. And, he got his grandson back. I think that's what this was all about," Nick said.

"He's a nasty, powerful man. I almost feel sorry for Barry," Carol said.

"Don't be. Changing the subject, have I told you today how much I love you?"

"I think I would have remembered. Tell me again."

Carol wanted every day to end on a similar romantic note. She put her arms around her future husband's neck, all the while admiring the ruby ring that sparkled in the sunlight. She felt far richer than Nick's last client.

End

Searching for Rachel

List of Characters

Rachel Greene, a young wife and mother who suddenly disappears, leaving her husband Barry stranded at the marina on the family's houseboat. She's a talented artist and only child of Ezra and Maureen Rueben.

Barry Greene, Rachel's husband who works for her father selling real estate. Barry managed the Smithville, TN branch office until Rachel disappeared and was forced to relocate to Ocala FL, where he continues to sell real estate.

Jonathan, Rachel and Barry's six year-old son. He's the only grandchild of Ezra and Maureen Rueben.

Ezra Rueben, Rachel's wealthy father, a real estate tycoon in Nashville, TN. He's a man used to having things done his way. He lives in Smithville, TN just a mile away from Barry and Rachel in an exclusive community he developed.

Maureen Rueben, Rachel's mother. She is content to live in luxury and accepts the decisions made by her husband, Ezra. She is from a wealthy family and used to having servants help with the housework.

Jake, Jonathan's dog, a Wire Hair Terrier.

Nick Alexander, a private investigator from the Detroit area. He's visiting his girlfriend who lives in nearby Cookeville. He agrees to look into Rachel's disappearance (Hired by Ezra). Eventually he regrets taking the assignment.

Richard Standring

Carol Mayberry, Nick Alexander's girlfriend lives in Cookeville, TN. She and Nick have known each other for four years when he was hired by her company to do background checks on key employees.

Herschel Fielding, an older private investigator in New Orleans hired by Ezra Rueben. His contacts and wisdom are legendary. Loves good food and good cigars.

Odell Hickey, a dock assistant at the Hurricane marina and the only person to witness Rachel's departure.

Sheriff Bobby Joe Hanks, knows just about everyone and everything going on in DeKalb County. Rachel's disappearance continues to haunt him and he keeps tabs on the progress of the investigation frequently reviewing his notes in the computer.

Deputy Randy Cooper, a deputy sheriff with DeKalb County Sheriff's Dept. assigned to investigate Rachel's disappearance. He dislikes the heavy-handed requests Ezra Rueben makes on the sheriff's department. He's also the sheriff's nephew.

Billy Randall, a real estate agent in the Smithville office. He worked with Barry Greene.

Meredith Mayfield, a close friend of Rachel's. They were roommates at Vanderbilt Univ.

Keith Snyder, a car salesman who worked with Barry at one time in Nashville. They still keep in touch.

Liz Miller, a sexy waitress at the Huddle House in Nashville. Formerly Lucille Fontaine, from Baton Rouge,

Searching for Rachel

LA. She is attractive and foxy. Seeks a chance for a better life and accepts the challenge when it comes along.

Mrs. Pearlman, an elderly widow in Ocala, Fl who is a part-time babysitter for Jonathan.

Harold Davis, a worthless, drunken private investigator in New Orleans hired by Barry.

Dooley, a taxi driver in New Orleans, who also works part-time for Herschel Fielding.

Reggie Burgoins, a pimp and drug dealer in New Orleans. Considered to be a dangerous man. He is also compassionate toward the prostitutes in his employ. And, he's an old Army buddy of Barry Greene from another life. They still keep in touch.

Monique, "Goldie" is a 42 year-old hooker who works for Reggie in New Orleans.

Sophie, a 16 year-old black girl who works in the kitchen, and cleans for Reggie, at The Lodge.

Amanda "Mandy" McBride, a private investigator who works for her father's agency in Ocala, FL. Frequently pretends to be a travel agent as a disguise.

Charles McBride, owns a private investigative agency in Ocala. Hired by Ezra Rueben to watch Barry's activity.

Author's note: With a long list of characters, it's easy to become confused with one or two names, after putting the book down for a period of time. I decided that having a quick reference might be helpful to the reader.

Richard Standring

About the Author

Richard Standring has written three other mysteries, *Dangerous Dancing*, *Dangerous Relationships* and *Dangerous Encounters* using Nick Alexander as the main character. He has also written a collection of short stories, poems and essays, *Somewhere Along the Way*.

   He contends that fiction mirrors real-life situations with a few "what ifs" to get his interest focused on a given event. He also contends that once the characters are established, they help in developing the story, as it moves along, using appropriate dialog. The end of the story always surprises him, as much as it does his readers, adding to his continued passion for writing. The ending should always pay off in a surprise.

   An avid reader, part-time golfer and gardener, Richard resides part of the year in Pembroke, MA and part of the year exploring other parts of the South. He lived in the Cookeville, TN area for 13 years and knows that part of the country well. For 30 years he was a private pilot. He retired from industrial magazine publishing in 1992.

   Readers can reach him with comments on the Internet by going to: marciamaggie@yahoo.com.